S0-AFO-016

BORDER SON

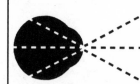

This Large Print Book carries the
Seal of Approval of N.A.V.H.

BORDER SON

WITHDRAWN

SAMUEL PARKER

THORNDIKE PRESS
A part of Gale, a Cengage Company

A Cengage Company

Farmington Hills, Mich • San Francisco • New York • Waterville, Maine
Meriden, Conn • Mason, Ohio • Chicago

Dunn Public Library

Copyright © 2019 by Samuel Parker.
Thorndike Press, a part of Gale, a Cengage Company.

ALL RIGHTS RESERVED
This book is a work of fiction. Names, characters, places, and incidents are the product of the author's imagination or are used fictitiously. Any resemblance to actual events, locales or persons, living or dead, is coincidental.
Thorndike Press® Large Print Christian Mystery.
The text of this Large Print edition is unabridged.
Other aspects of the book may vary from the original edition.
Set in 16 pt. Plantin.

LIBRARY OF CONGRESS CIP DATA ON FILE.
CATALOGUING IN PUBLICATION FOR THIS BOOK
IS AVAILABLE FROM THE LIBRARY OF CONGRESS

ISBN-13: 978-1-4328-6484-2 (hardcover alk. paper)

Published in 2019 by arrangement with Revell Books, a division of Baker Publishing Group

Printed in the United States of America
1 2 3 4 5 6 7 23 22 21 20 19

Man has places in his heart which do not yet exist, and into them enters suffering, in order that they may have existence.

— Léon Bloy

AUTHOR NOTE

Writing about a culture that I am not a part of was always going to be a dangerous proposition, especially in this day and age. My love and interest for the southwest and for Mexico comes from an unknown source. I am fascinated by the people, the myths, and the environment. If I have done a disservice to any of these during the writing of this book, it was never my intent.

Roberto, Camilla, and all the inhabitants of Nuevo Negaldo are not to be interpreted as caricatures of an entire people, but individuals. If anything, I wanted to represent the relentless devotion to family, an aspect of Mexican and Latino culture that I admire.

I am in debt to the works of Dan Slater (*Wolf Boys*), Luis Alberto Urrea (*The Devil's Highway, Across the Wire: Life and Hard Times on the Mexican Border*), Charles Bowden (*Murder City, Down By the River, El*

Sicario: Confessions of a Cartel Hit Man), Yuri Herra (*Signs Preceding the End of the World*), and Alfredo Corchado (*Midnight in Mexico*) as well as countless other authors who have written on the Drug Wars along the southern border. I will also freely admit that Felipe may be a little too indebted to Graham Greene (*The Power and the Glory*).

I am also indebted to my friend Sylvia Villalobos Everitt, who answered a slew of major and minor questions concerning Mexican-American culture, always willing to help steer me in the right direction as far as customs and language. If I made any mistakes or blunders in this book, it is due to not asking enough questions which I am sure she would have gladly answered.

At the end of the day, I wanted to write a story about *family,* set in a part of the world that inspires my imagination. To that end, I ask for your grace.

DRAMATIS PERSONAE

Ed Kazmierski
Tyler Kazmierski
Camilla Ibanez
Father Felipe
Agent Lomas
The Owner
Julio — coyote
Juan — migrant
Luis — migrant

Los Diablo
Roberto Ibanez
Miguel
Adan

Cartel
Hector Salazar — plaza boss
El Aguila — Cartel boss
El Matacerdos — sicario
Arturio
Vicente

1

The sun was cresting the low eastern hills of Nuevo Negaldo as the rusted Buick made its way through the still-sleeping town. A street sweeper turned his head and crossed himself as the car passed. It moved steadily, pushed neither by schedule nor fear of discovery. No one would dare watch it, and no one would dare talk.

Roberto Ibanez had driven this route before, so often that his mind would normally drift to the tune of the *narcocorrido* playing on the car's radio. But today was different. He was focused. Miguel sat in the passenger seat dozing, his head against the tinted window, his sleep apnea abated only when the car's suspension jolted.

The town gave way to the high desert scrub and emptiness. They drove into the sunrise, the day's story just beginning.

His left hand on the wheel, with the other Roberto rolled a coin through his fingers.

The image of Our Lady of Guadalupe on one side, script on the other.

Our Lady of Guadalupe
Help All Those Who Invoke
Thee in Their Necessities
Help Me to Alleviate All the Suffering
and Misfortunes in the World

Back and forth the coin rolled, back and forth his thoughts vacillated with the movement. His fate oscillating in his hand. He could not make up his mind.

Miles from Nuevo Negaldo the car stopped, kicking up dust that blew through the sagebrush. The doors opened and Roberto and Miguel got out. They walked around the back of the car and opened the trunk. Miguel stretched his back and yawned.

In the trunk were two men.

Roberto reached in and pulled out the first man. Then the second. Crammed in like sardines, their legs numb and asleep, the victims were unable to support their weight and they crumpled to the ground.

Each hostage had their hands bound behind their back with duct tape, one strip across their mouths, another across their eyes. The first captive was shorter, his

Mayan heritage darkening his skin and stunting his height. The other was a gringo.

"Miguel, you take him," Roberto said as he pushed the bound Mexican.

Miguel simply nodded and went to work.

Several yards off the road, Miguel forced the man down to his knees, drew a 9mm from his belt, aimed it at the back of the man's head, and pulled the trigger.

The Mexican fell against the desert floor, his feet spasming against rock as the blood left his body. Miguel fired two more shots into the dying form and then stretched his back again. Violence before breakfast was hard work.

Still standing behind the car, Roberto looked down at the coin in his hand. Our Lady looked up at him from the silver surface. He put the coin in his pocket as he whispered into the gringo's ear.

"Listen. I am going to shoot you. You will not die. It will hurt like hell, but fall forward and don't move. It is the best I can do."

The gringo tipped his blindfolded and gagged head, his breaths becoming more hurried and laborious through his nostrils.

Roberto grabbed the man's shirt above the left shoulder and pulled down, tearing the fabric and exposing the gringo's skin. Reaching into the trunk, he took a half-empty bottle of tequila and doused his victim's back, then took a swig of the remaining drops and threw the empty bottle on the ground.

Miguel returned to the car, tucking the gun into his overexerted waistband.

Roberto looked back with vacant eyes. "My turn."

Miguel got back into the Buick to enjoy the show from the comforts of the air-conditioned interior. Roberto pushed the gringo out to the killing ground. Just past the first victim, he forced the man down to his knees. He drew his pistol, ejected the magazine, removed one of the hollow point bullets, and replaced it with a ball round. He jammed the clip back into the pistol and chambered it.

"Be strong, *mi amigo,*" he whispered.

One shot into the man's back and the gringo fell. Roberto stepped over him, gun pointed down, and fired two quick rounds. He holstered the gun in his belt, then crossed himself. Turning back to the car, Roberto walked to the driver's door, got in, and drove back to Nuevo Negaldo.

2

The first shot had thrown Tyler forward, smashing his face into the dirt. Excruciating pain stabbed into his back and beat with his quickened pulse. Dust filled his nose as he sucked in against the tape over his mouth. His ears were ringing, left deaf by the two shots that had ricocheted off the hardpan next to his head. He felt the earth spinning beneath his masked eyes, the vertigo trapping his own thoughts inside his head, isolated from the world.

Inhale.

Exhale.

Pain.

The stabbing turned into burning and he could feel his blood pooling beneath him from his shoulder. The bullet had passed through, into the rock, burrowing a hole into the earth which now drank from him. The ringing in his ears slowly subsided, replaced by the desert silence. The only sound was his labored nasal breaths. He may have passed out or may have been aware. Roberto could have shot him five minutes ago or five hours, he could not tell.

The heat of the sun scorched his back.

Summoning his strength, Tyler tried to roll over but was stopped halfway by the lifeless body that lay next to him. He could feel his hair, wet, and didn't know if it was his own blood or Ignacio's. Tyler kicked at the body and grunted. No response. He kicked again.

Dead.

Ignacio had been tough. Smart. He had taken the beatings the night before quietly. Ignacio thought they would let him go. Now his mind was free of the burden of wondering. But then again, Tyler didn't expect it to end this way either.

The sun traversed the sky, but his only notice of it was the intensity of heat on him, baking him. The pain in his wound slowly numbed as the nerves exhausted themselves. He felt like a brick, his shoulder melding with the stones.

Time passed.

He heard a car approach, its four cylinders sounding as if only two still had life. It shuddered to a stop some distance away. Tyler heard a door open and close, then footsteps to his side. With a quick pull, the tape was ripped from his eyes and he was blinded by sunlight. His mouth was soon released and he sucked in air.

A small man squatted next to him, and as he poured water out of a bottle into his mouth, it ran down his cheeks. The man then poured some over Tyler's hair and neck, cooling him down. With a pocketknife, the man freed Tyler's hands.

"Can you get up?" he asked with a thick accent.

"I don't know."

"Well, then, I must drag you."

The man grabbed Tyler's good arm and began to drag him toward his car. Tyler attempted to get his legs under him, but only succeeded in pushing his heels into the dirt, helping what little he could to move his body through the dust. The man pushed him into the passenger seat of an old Ford Falcon and slammed the door. Tyler watched as the man walked over to Ignacio, bent down, and examined the body. He then kicked up the ground where Tyler had been lying and rolled Ignacio onto it.

Soon the man returned to the car, put it in drive, and headed back toward town.

"Who are you?" Tyler whispered. He felt on the verge of an abyss and a willingness

17

with each passing second to fall into it.

"Felipe. Father Felipe."

"How did you find me?"

"Roberto."

Tyler's eyes grew heavy. The throbbing in his shoulder returned. Words became exhausting. "He trying for sainthood?"

Felipe laughed to himself. "No . . . he will never be that."

"Well, he's one today."

"Yes. Maybe just for today."

Blackness overcame him as the sun shone bright over the desert east of Nuevo Negaldo.

3

Roberto sat below the oscillating fan nailed to a dark corner of one of the grimiest cantinas in Nuevo Negaldo. Miguel was busy throwing money at one of the women smuggled up from the poor villages in the south to dance on the tables and then be discarded when the next batch arrived. Roberto sipped his beer and eyed all the men who came and went, the bartender, the girls as they moved in and out of the back room. His anxiety had risen with each mile they drove between the killing ground and Nuevo Negaldo. He had second-guessed himself the whole way back, and had considered turning around and killing Tyler where he had left him.

But by this point, Felipe had most likely found Tyler and taken him into hiding.

That was the agreement.

It was a dangerous game that he had started — this demented plan to repay a debt — and there were few that Roberto could trust to help him execute it. Felipe was one of them.

His uncle. He could trust him.

He thought he could trust Miguel, but just to be sure, he had gone through the motions and left his compadre in the dark. Miguel was an ox, and dumb as rocks, and if he knew the plan Roberto had laid out for Tyler to get out of Mexico, under Salazar's nose, then he might just tell the wrong person out of sheer stupidity. Miguel was good muscle. He was good because he didn't have many thoughts slowing down his actions.

They had been ordered to take Tyler and Ignacio out that morning and kill them. Hector Salazar, the plaza boss, had ordered it, and when the order came down, there was no question. Roberto and Miguel had arrived at Salazar's hacienda, watched as some men loaded the two doomed souls in the back of the car, and then drove out. They had done it before, many times, and the routine was one thing Roberto hoped would aid in his plan. Having Miguel witness him shooting the American would not provide his dumb friend with anything out of the ordinary to report.

The only thing that could expose the plan

was Tyler himself. Either he was already dead out in the desert, Felipe had picked him up, or . . .

The sunlight coming through the open door would dim in shadow when a patron would enter. Each time Roberto found himself holding his breath in case an unlikely event would happen — one of Hector's men dragging in a half-alive Tyler and demanding an explanation.

It never did.

The last part of the plan was simple and complex at the same time.

All that remained was to get him across the border.

It was this last point, waiting out in the future, that unnerved him to no end. The border. Tyler could not simply walk across. He could not drive across. All roads north were watched and monitored by Salazar's men and informants on both sides of the border. Even some of the US Customs guys were on the payroll. They would find Tyler. And if they did, not only would Tyler take a bullet in the head, but Roberto could also go down. They would probably kill Miguel too, just for being in the wrong place at the wrong time.

Miguel looked over to Roberto, a half-drunken smirk on his face, oblivious to the potential danger his partner had put him in. He laughed and turned back to his entertainment.

The last part would be difficult.

It hinged on one person now. One person who had no idea what she was being asked to do, but would do what Roberto asked because she loved him and would do what she could to help him. She always did, and even though there were few in this life that Roberto cared about, he cared about his mother above all others.

He would ask her to make a phone call, and the outcome of that call would determine how much longer he had to bear the anxiety of his actions. The phone call. It had popped into his mind just as quickly as had the idea of getting his uncle Felipe to go retrieve the body. A memory of something Tyler had said, way back, presented itself before him as clear as the desert sun. If there was anyone who would risk helping Tyler, it was the person his mother was to call. And if they didn't help, then Roberto might as well just drag Tyler back out to the wasteland and shoot him dead.

He felt a twinge of guilt, involving his mother and uncle in this. Felipe at least knew the brutality of the world, but his mother seemed to float untouched by its harsh realities. And even though they were oblivious to the peril circling around them, he justified himself by thinking that he was doing a noble deed. A deed they always wished he would do. To be a good man, not a hood, a tool of Salazar and the Cartel. Perhaps this would be the only good thing he would ever do. He couldn't do it alone, he needed the help of others to make it happen. It just couldn't get done fast enough.

4

Iglesia de Señor de la Misericordia was on the western side of Nuevo Negaldo. The church was built from river stone over a hundred years before. It had been built on the remains of the mission that the Apaches had burned down. The church stood in memoriam of the few brave souls who survived then and since, those who scratched out an existence in this barren land. The stone looked wet, its glossy tone a contrast to the sandblasted adobes, as if the building shed continual tears for her children running wayward through the streets.

Father Felipe had spent his entire life here. His childhood spent wandering the arroyos and hillsides, his teenage years doing more unwholesome things. But once a man, he took Holy Orders and had ministered to the people of Nuevo Negaldo the best he could. The border had always been dangerous and Felipe could think of no better place to ply his trade.

It was home.

These were his streets, his people, and he loved them both.

Iglesia de Señor de la Misericordia was his refuge from the violence, and it was a refuge for many in these barbaric times. Most of the regulars were old women lighting candles for hooligan grandchildren caught up in the crime of the city. Many of their men were either in the north earning remittances for their family, in jail, or dead before they had the opportunity to be grandfathers. And when they came back with enough money to return, they got out of Nuevo Negaldo as fast as they could. They would return, gather what was left of their families, and go to a place where they wouldn't be caught in the cross fire of the rival factions.

Felipe was old enough to have witnessed the full progression of many *cholos.* From baptism to altar boy to gangbanger, then a body on the street riddled with bullets. The procession of the coffin would lead out of the church to the cemetery, another life gone to the angels. He would look at the new altar boys and see in their faces the next round of *sicarios* and victims, and yet he carried on as a beacon of hope to whoever may come to the church for help, no matter what they might have done.

He was not an idealist or a romantic. He knew that these boys had few options. They were the poor of Mexico and would be the illegals of America. What more could they hope for? He would pray for them, help them where he could. But he also knew they would thank him for his kindness and then inflict unmerciful harm on another the next day. He didn't attend to them for who they might become, and didn't refuse them for what they had done. He simply offered his assistance as it was required.

And so it was a natural extension for him to be sitting in a dark cell below one of the chapels in the church, applying a cool rag to the feverish head of a gringo who had been shot in the back. As natural as pouring holy water over an infant's head or the casket of a dead drug runner. They were all the same in God's eyes.

Roberto had called, and Felipe had answered.

He needed no explanation, and for the most part did not want to hear one. He was human, after all, and knowing too much was always a risk to his decency. He prayed not to be judgmental, for he knew he could descend that path easily enough if he wasn't careful. No. Better to aid the sick no matter what they might have done, all were deserving.

Amen.

The small cot the gringo slept on was wet with sweat, the man's fever not abating. Something else was driving the man's pain. Not just the gunshot, but something else. Most likely drugs, his body raging for the chemicals it was used to. Not much to be done for that but keep him cool and change the dressings. Withdrawal wouldn't kill the man, but it would not be pleasant. It was a good thing he was rarely conscious.

A man entered the room with a bag, and Felipe got up from the stool, offering it to him. The man sat down and began to examine the patient, and Felipe stood and walked out the narrow doorway, up the stone steps into the chapel, and closed the old wooden door behind him. The door was decorated with a large retablo of Shadrach, Meshach, and Abednego in the furnace, a fitting cover for the man burning in the cell below.

Felipe walked out of the chapel, into the nave of the church, and stepped to the front doors. The sky was clear and the sun was raining its light down on the city. It was a beautiful day. A beautiful day to help anyone who asked.

5

Roberto left Miguel at the bar and headed west on Revolución Street. The sun was beginning its descent and its rays beat down on the concrete and dust of the city. He stopped and got some food from a takeout and continued on. He slowly walked past the garage where some of his crew would hang out if there was no action to be had. He saw a couple under the hood of a car tweaking on hoses, and they looked up and he nodded back.

He thought of walking in and telling Adan what he had done. Adan ran Los Diablos in Nuevo Negaldo. It was he who gave the orders to go up to Salazar's that morning and carry out the execution. Los Diablos were subcontractors in violence. But just as he couldn't tell Miguel what the score was, there was no way he could tell Adan.

He felt uneasy on the street, just as uneasy as he had in the bar, as if at any moment somebody would jump out and put a bullet in his head. He wasn't scared of dying; he had seen too much of it to be spooked by the mystery of death. What made him nervous were all the things the Cartel did to people who crossed them before they killed them. Nuevo Negaldo was littered with the evidence of their cruelty.

Roberto liked the feeling of others averting their eyes, changing their pace, stepping aside, when he walked down the streets. But these same people would look the other way if the Cartel decided to make an example out of him. A bullet would be a quick death and he would make sure that was how he would go out. He put his hand behind his back, beneath his top-buttoned shirt, and felt the grip of the pistol lodged in his belt. Ready at a moment's notice.

He was quick with a gun and had practiced more than any other cholo in Nuevo Negaldo. It was accuracy that mattered, not volume. All these other suckers held their guns like they did in the movies. Not him. He was fast, steady, and accurate. He was the Doc Holliday of the Nuevo Negaldo thugs. It's why Adan kept him on tap for work like this morning's. When the Cartel gave Adan an order, Adan knew that he could count on Roberto to get it done.

But now he had crossed Salazar even if Salazar hadn't realized it. If Tyler survived the wound that morning, Roberto could not say he messed up. A gunman who could not kill a man at close range was of little use to anyone. Adan would have his hand forced to have Roberto removed.

And Los Diablos had no retirement plan.

Bored and wound up, he headed to the cinder-block home he shared with his mother. She was at work across the border and sometimes didn't come home until close to midnight.

He walked in and locked the door behind him. From the refrigerator he grabbed a drink, placed a chair facing the door, and sat down. He pulled out the gun and rested it on his leg with one hand, tipping the bottle with the other, watching the door.

He would not let them take him.

And he was going to make sure they weren't ever going to take him by surprise.

The curtain on the barred window by the door moved slowly with the gentle breeze from outside. He could hear the voices of kids playing soccer in the alley two doors down. Their playing spoke of an alternate reality in the streets of the border town.

His nerves were slowly settling as he rocked in his chair, the time moving on from the incident of the morning. After an hour, he pulled his cell phone out of his pocket and called his uncle.

"Hola," said a familiar voice on the line.

"Did you do the pickup?"

"Yes."

"Alive?"

"Yes."

"Hidden away?"

"Yes. It is safe from sight."

"Bueno," Roberto said and hung up the phone.

He stood and walked to the window, careful not to expose too much of his body to the glass in the event a shooter outside was waiting for a chance, but the street had emptied out as dusk set in.

His mother would be home in a few hours. He would ask her to make the call tomorrow.

6

Camilla Ibanez drove her old Honda toward the border crossing, idled in line for almost an hour in the late morning light, and then headed up to the restaurant she worked at in Hurtado, New Mexico. The US side was vastly different than the Mexican side, as if all the Americans who were able to had fled the little town, leaving behind just those who were bound by the immobility of their trailer homes. Nuevo Negaldo, south of the border, was a large concrete and tin community of thousands of Mexicans, Hurtado on the north scarcely more than a few hundred.

Camilla had spent her whole life moving between the two countries. Her mother had given her a tangible gift at her birth, having delivered her in an El Paso delivery room, making Camilla a dual citizen simply by being born a few miles north of the border. Growing up, she had crossed the border every morning for school and eventually work, but always returning at night to her home in Mexico. She had lived for a year in El Paso, but the cost was too expensive compared to Juarez and she found herself moving back in time. When Roberto was born, she made sure she was north when he was delivered.

Eventually her mother got sick and moved back with family in Nuevo Negaldo, and Camilla followed her, Roberto in tow. In her mind's eye she thought that it would be better for Roberto to grow up away from Juarez, but it seems that bad mojo is not bound to large cities alone.

She pulled into the parking lot of the restaurant just before noon and locked her car. She would spend the next twelve hours feeding border patrol agents and medical tourists, each with their own interests in the crossing. She had her regulars that she enjoyed seeing, some on each shift, and some of the old folks once a month when their prescriptions needed to be renewed. Her Mexico supplied more than illegal narcotics to the drug-crazed Americans. There were plenty of gringo baby boomers in search of affordable pain relief as well.

To her, though, it mattered little.

North of the border she could earn a bit

more, the tips in US currency carried more weight, and she liked the simplicity of American business. She had no idea if the owner of the establishment had to pay the Cartel protection money, but she knew that she didn't have to kick in any of her wages for the service. Once back home, the money would stretch considerably farther and she lived rather comfortably. It just was the way it was, and had been her whole life, that most days she passed through the routine without thinking too much about her course in life.

Get up, go to work, drive home.

And worry.

Worry about Roberto. That was a full-time job in and of itself. She loved her son, just as much now as when he was born, but the worry racked her body like the pains of birthing the boy. She had done her best to raise him right, to raise him good, had prayed to the Blessed Mother to keep him straight, but somewhere along the road he had decided on a different path. A path that she imagined but never asked about. She did not want to know what he did, the things he did, the sins he committed. She did not want to lose the image of Roberto that she kept locked away in her heart.

But she worried.

She knew that one day he would not be there. That she would arrive home and she would be told that he was dead. That he was missing. That he was the one lying in the plaza, bullet ridden, or thrown onto Revolución Street dismembered and disfigured. Like so many mothers of Mexico, she worried about her son.

And so when Roberto had asked her to do this task for him, that what he was asking her to do was a "good thing, Mama, please," what could she do but concede, in the hopes that her son was doing the right thing. For the first time in a long time. And she had noticed a look in his face when he asked, not the cold stare of a man who had seen wicked things, but a subtle pleading of the eyes that reminded her of ages past.

So she agreed.

After the lunch crowd, she looked up at the clock and saw it was 1:35. This seemed like a good time to do what Roberto, her son, had asked her to do.

Camilla walked to the back room and picked up the phone. She pulled from her pocket a note and punched in the number written on the paper. The phone rang several times and she was ready to hang up when it was picked up.

"Hello?"

"Yes," she said, her English touched with a Spanish accent. "May I speak with Mr. Kazmierski?"

"This is him."

"Good." Camilla looked down on the paper and began to recite the script. "This is concerning your son, Tyler. He needs you in Hurtado, New Mexico, as soon as possible —"

"Now wait a second —"

"Check in to the Plaza Motel, and come to La Casa de Irma when you arrive. It is the restaurant across the street. Ask for Ibanez," she finished, putting the paper down.

"Please . . . wait . . . ," the voice said.

Camilla listened, her breath filtering down through the mouthpiece.

"What is this all about? I haven't heard from Tyler in years. Who is this?"

The questions kept coming. Camilla raised the paper to her face again and prepared to speak the line that Roberto had written on the bottom of the page. She had no idea what it meant, but he had told her to use it if the man she called doubted her.

"Remember Denver . . . It's like that. Please come."

She hung up the phone before the man on the other end could question her about the comment.

Camilla walked back to the dining area and started prepping for dinner. Her mind kept going back to the conversation she had with Roberto, about this man Tyler he mentioned, about the man's father who needed to come down and pick him up. He had assured her this was a good thing, a noble thing, not one of his hoodlum rackets, and thus she agreed to help him out. But placing the call had unnerved her, as if she was participating in a secret meeting of criminal minds.

Now, she just had to wait for a man to arrive asking for "Ibanez" and let Roberto know. For now all she had to worry about was doing her work and making it through the day.

And Roberto. She always worried about him.

7

There is a fate worse than shunning.

The old-world religious orders would turn their eyes from the offending member, excluding them from their community. It is an active gesture. A physical turning, a forcing from sight of the person who has violated whatever covenant may have existed. To do so means, at the least, acknowledging the existence of the person.

But to progress further to the point where the mind's eye no longer sees the individual, where memories can no longer be recalled, where the conscious self has no twinge of recollection when the face is presented before it, this, the *Great Erasing,* is death to the guilty.

Even Cain was remembered.

Was marked for remembrance.

Exile is better than being tossed onto the scrap heap of oblivion.

But for all intents and purposes, this was

the realm to which Edward Kazmierski had pushed any and every thought of his son Tyler. His mind did not connect the past to his daily life, and each day would securely seal the vault of memory one more notch. Life went on.

He got up, went to work, came home, went to bed.

That was it. All was done without thought of his progeny.

But now with one phone call, it had all come rushing back.

He hung up the receiver and walked out the front screen door and sat on the front porch, his chair leaning back as he stared out across the farm fields that his family had owned before his father sold out. This was his father's land, and his father's before him. But in the new America it would never be Ed's.

In the sale, the family had kept the house. Ed had used his skills and some of his father's money to open the appliance shop in Jennison, Kansas. It was located on the west end of Main Street, next to a Dairy Queen that kept more unreliable hours than Ed did. His was the last building you would pass before hitting the high prairie that would eventually become Colorado.

Ed's own young family moved in when

his parents went to live out their years in Tampa. But the serenity of a new family in a country house didn't last long and withered like crops in a drought.

One day Sally, Ed's wife, left for a better life out in California without bothering to tell anybody where she was going. That had been it. Ed got a call from the school that his son hadn't been picked up. He left the shop, picked up the boy, and drove home to find the place abandoned. A note on the kitchen table simply told Ed that Sally went west, that he should not bother following her, and to tell their son that she loved him but had to go and find herself.

This empty house became their new normal. Then a few years later, Tyler was gone, and a new kind of emptiness became Ed's reality.

And then today, the phone rang.

The call unnerved him more than he could have imagined it would. Today was the first day in a long, long time that he had thought of Tyler. Ed tried to count the years. His son must be twenty-six now.

Ed stood and walked over to his truck, got in, and fired up the engine. He needed to drive as a cathartic exercise. To feel the physical acceleration in order to keep pace with his racing thoughts.

41

8

Ed drove down the dirt drive until he hit asphalt. He accelerated on the road as the late summer wheat fields whipped past his open window. He drifted out on the back roads of the high prairie, driving to the barely audible sounds of Johnny Cash on the radio, the hot air blowing against his face.

He drove on.

Finally, after calming his nerves and driving for nearly an hour, he turned around and headed back. He pulled into the gas station on the eastern edge of Jennison. The town was a small farming community that was slowly receding into history. Most of the other family farms had been sold off to agribusinesses, kids never came back from college, and no new blood ever considered planting roots.

He got out of his truck, put the gas hose in his tank, and went in the store to pay for the fill-up. The old rust bucket could probably make it to New Mexico as long as he topped off the radiator more often than not. It still drove smooth. He would just have to baby it a bit.

Ed caught himself mid-thought.

Why was he even considering it?

Why was the feasibility of a drive to New Mexico even crossing his mind? A couple years ago Ed received a phone call from the El Paso jail. Tyler said he needed bail. Ed simply hung up the phone. And that was it. There was no grand fight, no huge come-to-Jesus meeting when each had said words too strong to take back. They had simply walked in separate directions, and as men do, stubbornly refused to look back.

So why now? Why bother to think about Tyler now?

Ed paid the clerk and walked out of the store back toward his vehicle. The local sheriff pulled in beside him. A hand waved out of the open driver's window. Ed nodded in reply.

"Hey, Tom," Ed said as he went to pump the gas.

"Ed. Glad I saw you. I was about ready to head over to your place."

The sheriff got out of his car and the two men talked casually over the truck bed.

"What you need?"

"I got a phone call today from a fed. He was asking about you."

"About me?"

"Rather, about your boy."

Ed could feel his hand tremor on the gas pump. He wanted to go back before the phone call, before his wandering thoughts about Tyler. Before all the *past* was hauled to the *present.*

"Tyler?" Ed said. "Why would they be asking about Tyler?"

"Didn't say. Just asked if your number was current, seems like they been trying to get ahold of you this afternoon."

"Yeah, I've just been out driving."

"No need to give me an excuse," Tom said with a smile. "I wouldn't answer them either if I could avoid it."

"What do you think they want?"

"No idea. But I assume if they are looking for Tyler, well, it can't be anything you'd want to hear about."

Ed nodded. The pump quit at twenty bucks and he put the hose back up and sealed the cap. Tom had been the sheriff in Jennison for decades, and it was usually him who brought Tyler home in the back of his cruiser, or called Ed when Tyler was at the police station for whatever stupid situation

44

he had got himself into. Ed always thanked Tom for keeping Tyler out of the court-house, and Tom always felt sorry for Ed having to deal with a miscreant child.

"So what did you tell them?"

"Just that I'd find you, give you the message," Tom said, handing over a piece of notepaper with a name and number on it. Ed looked at it. "Probably best to call him back before they send the black helicopters out for you."

Tom opened the door of his patrol car and put a foot in, then looked back at Ed. "Call him collect. You know . . . just because." He got in the car and drove off.

Ed followed suit and headed back home, his life having gotten incredibly more complicated in just the past couple of hours.

9

Ed pulled into the gravel drive, parked, and went inside. He fished a beer out of the fridge, pulled the phone off the wall, and sat at the kitchen table. He took out the paper that Tom had given him and looked at the number, punching it into the keypad.

It rang several times and then was answered by a switchboard operator.

"Agent Lomas, please."

"One minute, sir."

He waited on hold until the interminable music was silenced.

"This is Agent Lomas," a voice said.

"Yes, this is Ed Kazmierski. I was given a message that you've been trying to reach me."

"Yes, yes," Lomas said. Ed imagined the agent on the other end of the line suddenly straightening up at his desk and shuffling papers. "I have some questions I hope you can answer for me."

"I'll do what I can." Ed took a sip of beer.

"I'm afraid it's a pretty urgent matter."

"It's about Tyler, isn't it?"

"Uh, yes. Yes it is," Lomas said.

Ed closed his eyes and exhaled slowly. He could feel the weight begin to descend onto his shoulders. The sucking-down feeling that he felt when his life was slipping into chaos. When his wife had left. When he was a single parent dealing with Tyler's hooliganism. He took for granted how easy life was without these burdens, and now it was back. It was returning, against all his efforts over the years to detach himself from it. He could feel the pull.

"So, what'd he do?" Ed said, more defeated than inquisitive.

"I'm afraid I'm not allowed to divulge too many details of an ongoing investigation, Mr. Kazmierski, but I'll be straight with you."

"I'd appreciate that."

"Your son has been involved in some major drug-running operations through Nuevo Negaldo into New Mexico. The DEA was tracking him for several years. He wasn't a main concern for us. Just a hired mule for the Cartel. A couple weeks ago, we got word that a major shipment was being planned. Your son was part of that shipment. But then everything went black. Simply disappeared."

"Disappeared?"

"Disappeared. Tyler, along with another man he was working with. They left Nuevo Negaldo with the shipment. No one has seen them since. They simply dropped off the grid. Word coming from Mexico is that the shipment was dumped, and the mules were removed from their positions."

"Removed?"

"I apologize for my insensitivity, Mr. Kazmierski." Lomas paused on the line. "It's possible that Tyler went back to Nuevo Negaldo. When it comes to a shipment as large as this one is rumored to have been, the Cartel doesn't leave room for mistakes. If he did go back, it more than likely would not have ended well for him."

Ed's hand began to tremble and the sensation ran up his arm to his throat, his face, his eyes. "When?"

"The shipment went missing five days ago."

"Five?"

"Yes."

The phone call this morning. *"Your son, Tyler. He needs you."* Was he alive? He felt his guts turning, the feeling growing along with another. Worry? Concern? His head swam. It was a split-second decision not to bring up the phone call. Something the woman said had stuck in his subconscious and kept poking at a part of his mind that he had buried.

"So . . . what do you want from me?" Ed said.

"Were you in contact with your son? Any letters, email, phone calls over the past year?"

"I'm afraid not." It wasn't really a lie. "We had sort of a falling out a ways back. Once he first got into this drug mess. Started stealing money from me, pawning some things. I kicked him out."

"How long ago was that?"

"About six years, I guess. I know he got arrested in El Paso a couple years ago. He called me from jail. Wanted me to post bail for him. I refused. That was the last time I heard from him."

"Nothing since then?"

Ed sipped his beer again. "No, nothing."

"All right then, Mr. Kazmierski. Please give me a call if you should think of anything that might be useful. Anything at all. Even small details help in these types of investigations."

"Sure thing, Agent Lomas." He jotted down the number Lomas read off. "Can I ask you a question?"

"Shoot," Lomas said.

"Are you looking for Tyler or are you looking for the shipment?"

"Both. Tyler is a US citizen, of course . . . but that shipment is valuable not only to keep off the streets, but we don't want the Cartel up here looking for it. We prefer to keep their war south of the border."

"Thanks."

"For what?"

"Being honest," Ed said.

"Remember, if there is anything at all that comes to mind, no matter how insignificant, please call me."

"I will," Ed said and hung up the phone.

He breathed out as if the pressure of the world had built up inside his chest.

He brought the bottle up to his lips and finished it off, then ran his hands through his hair. "Good Lord, Tyler," he whispered, "what did you do?"

10

Lomas placed the receiver back in the cradle on his desk and let out a long sigh. He could feel the tension in his neck constricting down his spine. Looking for answers in dead ends, because the dead held all the answers.

He stood and walked to the window of his office that overlooked downtown El Paso. From the ninth floor of the building, he could see the border crossing into Juarez with its long train of vehicles backed up waiting to enter America. So much flowing back and forth, day in and day out, not only at this crossing but the almost fifty such checkpoints running from Brownsville to San Diego. He didn't need this headache. Loads got seized, dumped, skimmed every day. Salazar should know this. He should have contingencies and remedies on his side of the border. He should be using his enforcers to handle it. Not him. He didn't like sticking his neck out in these sorts of

51

Dunn Public Library

situations, and wanted nothing more than to tell him where to go, but he knew he couldn't.

He had made that deal a long time ago. Back when he needed money for the important things in life. The new wife, the new house, the new car. Now all three were gone, along with most of the money. But the hooks in him would never loosen.

He wanted a drink and a cigarette, but the office administrator would come down harder on him than the Cartel if they even caught a whiff of tobacco burning in his government-owned office.

He pulled the cell phone from his pants pocket and pushed a button. The speed dial worked quickly.

"Yeah, it's Lomas."

He waited a minute as if on hold.

Finally, a deep voice came on. "Yes?"

"No word on this side. No seizures of the size you're looking for."

"You'd know?" Salazar said.

"Yeah, I'd know. They wouldn't hide it, they couldn't keep the news quiet about it."

"What about the family?"

"Tyler's old man doesn't know anything. Hasn't spoken to him in years. Mother's in California, not involved."

"Are you sure?"

"Yeah. Mental health ward the past five years."

"The father. Jennison, Kansas?"

Lomas took another deep breath. The Cartel knew everything, but it still struck him cold when he was reminded of that fact. "Yes."

"Very well. I'll send someone up to double-check. Just to be thorough."

"I told you I'd handle this."

"Agent Lomas. You must understand. I always plan for any technicality. Consider them as just the contingency plan. As you might say . . . your backup."

"I don't need any backup. And you are taking unnecessary risks having your guys running around up here. It isn't safe for any of us."

"Are you lecturing me on how to run my business?"

"No . . . just saying that your boys aren't exactly subtle in how they handle things. Podunk, Kansas, isn't Nuevo Negaldo. You can't solve problems by spraying bullets into people."

Salazar's silence on the other end was deafening.

"I'll get a tap on Kazmierski's phone. Other than that, the guy is cold. A waste of time."

"I am sure that will be confirmed."

Lomas gritted his teeth as he covered the microphone with his hand. He wanted to punch the wall. Salazar sending people north was a stupid move. "Normally, if you want a piece of information, it's best not to kill the only people who have it."

The phone went dead.

Lomas pocketed the phone and his frustration boiled over. He had little remorse for being in the pocket of the Cartel. Life was expensive and the government pay was almost insulting. What he hated was that his fortunes were tied to a person like Salazar. Salazar was impulsive. He didn't use his head and it was rumored that was causing issues with the Cartel boss. Salazar was going to get them all killed if he kept messing up. The lost load was his responsibility. Killing Tyler and Ignacio before he recovered the goods was an idiotic move.

He needed fresh air. He felt like he would suffocate in his office.

Lomas took the elevator down to street level and walked down the block. He lit up and the nicotine calmed his nerves while his feet took him to a pub for a drink. Something in his gut was telling him things were going to get so much worse.

11

It would be a night of little sleep and fitful dreams on both sides of the border.

In Nuevo Negaldo, in two different locations of the city, two wayward sons drifted between the living and the dying.

Roberto had holed himself up all day at his mother's house. Miguel had been by before lunch and asked what was going on.

"Just sick," Roberto said.

"You need a doctor? You look awful."

"No, I'm fine."

"Seriously, bro, you look like you're having a heart attack."

"I said I'm fine, *pendejo*. Just leave me alone."

Miguel held up his hands and walked to the Spartan kitchen area, got himself a drink of Roberto's tequila, then headed out the front door. He came back around five and the two had the same conversation. The shadows on the walls had just shifted location.

"I'll swing by in the morning. Salazar wants us to drive over to Corralito tomorrow."

Corralito was an airstrip about forty miles south of Nuevo Negaldo. It was also a great place for someone to execute a hit. The airstrip was isolated from all civilization, a redundant feature, as there were few in Mexico who would willingly pry into Salazar's business. Roberto felt his guts tighten and the cold sweat return to his forehead.

"Why does he want us down there?"

"He has everyone going. I guess some *político* from Mexico City is flying in and Salazar wants to flex some muscle."

It made sense. But even so, he would never know if Salazar was aware of his double-cross right up to the moment that they blew his head off.

"Okay," Roberto said, steeling himself, "I'll be ready to go."

Roberto paced the house until after midnight when his mother finally arrived home. She walked in and went to kiss his cheek, but he stepped aside.

"So did you make the call?"

"Yes, this afternoon."

"And?"

"And what?"

"Is he coming down?"

"He didn't say. But I gave the message."

Roberto paced faster. His patience had always been scarce, but now he felt like he was ready to claw out of his own skin.

"What's going on, Roberto? Tell me."

"Nothing, Mama, nothing."

"Roberto, tell me," Camilla said sternly.

"The less you know, the better. If the man you called comes to see you, send him on to Felipe as soon as possible and do not ask questions."

"Felipe? Why is Felipe involved in this?"

"Stop asking questions, Mama. Please! Just stop."

Camilla looked dumbfounded, her face growing pale as the worry slowly started setting into her features. "Okay. Okay, Roberto. I will do as you say."

12

Time had become untraceable for Tyler as he drifted in and out of consciousness. He could still taste the dirt in his mouth from the desert floor, the sticky residue binding his eyes, though the tape had been removed by the priest when he rolled him over in the desert. There were times that Tyler felt like he was back there. Bleeding out in the wasteland.

He lay naked in the dark. He could feel his shoulder burning as if he were lying on a pile of coals. He didn't have the energy to move, not even to shoo the flies away from his face as they would land lightly on his cheek, then on his nose.

He remembered waking in a fit of convulsion, nausea. The cold sweats despite the intolerable heat. He clawed at the hand that held a washcloth to his forehead, scratching at it, begging for it to go away.

He had dreamt of death, just as he had

dreamt of a hit of something to make him float away from life, the lack of a fix driving his weakened mind rabid.

There had been a man, a light in his hand, washing the wound, pumping pills in his mouth, but they were not the type of pills that made him soar.

Through the hours of oblivion, Tyler had thought he heard the tolling of church bells, as if his soul was being pulled toward the gates of heaven. He thought he was going mad. There was only one place he knew his soul would drift, and it certainly wasn't up to meet St. Peter.

Tyler didn't know how many days it had been since he was taken out into the desert. It could have been yesterday. It could have been years ago.

In that state of bewilderment, he opened his eyes and gazed at the ceiling. His fever was gone, but he still lay in sweat-soaked sheets. His eyes tried to adjust to the dim light coming from a pane of glass high on the stone wall, and the room slowly came into focus. A brick closet, silent except for the flies. He was lying on a cot that creaked with each movement. His back was wet, and he wondered if he had bled through all the way to the floor. Sitting across from him near the door was a small Mexican. The man just stared at him with sympathy in his eyes.

"Where am I?" Tyler asked.

"Safe. You're safe now."

"Who are you?"

"Father Felipe. I brought you here almost two days ago. On request from Roberto."

Roberto. The friend who had dragged him into the desert and shot him in the back. "Am I dying?"

"No. We have had this conversation three times before, Tyler. You are not dying. The wound in your back will not be the death of you. Roberto, it seems, knows exactly where to place a bullet."

The priest stood, walked over to the cot, and lifted the bandage a little to look at the wound.

"Roberto is a master. One little bit this way, he would have hit your subclavian artery. That would have been bad. The bullet he used came straight through, no debris. If you are going to get shot, Roberto is the one to do it. It was the only way he could keep you alive."

"So why are you keeping me here?"

"I am not keeping you here. You are free to go, anytime you like. But you would not make it a mile before you are picked up as a drunk or a vagrant. Then the Cartel will get you again, and this time, it will not be Roberto putting a bullet in your back."

Tyler's thoughts resisted his efforts to slow them down. He should have been dead. Was convinced wholeheartedly that he was going to die. When he was pulled from the car and heard Roberto's voice in his ear, he felt like a death row inmate getting a midnight pardon. But now what? He was still in Mexico with no conceivable hope of salvation except for the passing fancy of this priest. He couldn't rely on Roberto anymore. They were square. Even.

"What am I to do then, live here as your altar boy?"

Felipe smirked. "Ahh, gringo. Even in a time like this you cannot be grateful? I take a great risk keeping you here. Risk to my parishioners. Risk to myself."

"I didn't ask for any favors."

"No, but Roberto did."

"Why is that?"

"He is my nephew. And I know that someday, he will be in your position. Lying in the dust, bullets in his body. Perhaps by doing this I will secure the favor of God on his behalf. That when it happens, when his time comes, someone will pick him up and keep him from death."

"All right, padre."

"Yes . . . I guess it is *all right.*"

"So, what's the game plan?"

"My role here was to keep you alive. It is someone else's job to lead you out of Mexico. I have done my part."

"And whose job is that?"

"I am still waiting on that. You cannot go out alone, as I have said. You cannot simply walk across the border. The police, the border agents, even the cab drivers — many work for the Cartel now. You would not make it far. No. Your only chance is by leaving Nuevo Negaldo and making your way to America by some other way. Unfortunately, in your condition you will not make it on your own. You will need someone to practically carry your bones for you. Judging by the little I care to know of you, those volunteering on that list are very few."

Tyler chuckled, then broke into a cough that tortured his wound anew. "Yeah, you could say that."

"But perhaps there is one person who would do such a thing for you. At the least, if he would not, then we would know that no one will."

Tyler used all his strength and sat up on the cot. He placed his feet on the floor and watched the room momentarily spin before his eyes. His head swooned and then came back to balance. He looked at the priest.

"And who do you suggest that would be?"

"Your father."

Earlier that evening, a car had crossed the border in Juarez and proceeded north toward I-40. Before dawn it had cut the corners of the panhandles of Texas and Oklahoma and driven into Kansas. One man slept in the back seat while the other took his turn at the wheel. The sun started to skirt the eastern horizon when they saw the first sign for Jennison.

13

The next morning, Ed was in the back workroom at his shop, his thoughts buried deep in the small world of a washing machine motor. He was at ease working with machines. Solutions were straightforward. Wire to connector, *a* to *b,* give it some power, watch it do what it was supposed to do. It was a world that ran as it should, and when a machine broke down, it wasn't because it took off for a new life on the West Coast or pumped its insides full of drugs. It just broke down from old age.

It calmed his nerves, and after the information that had flooded his mind the day before, he needed this time to clear his head.

The bell over the front door rang and he could hear footsteps enter the building.

"Be right there!" he yelled. Ed put his tools down on the bench, wiped his hands off with a rag, and walked out to see his customer.

Two men stood in the store. A tall, skinny one was halfway to the front counter. The other larger one was standing by the front door like a bouncer at a nightclub. Ed could feel the tension in his neck rise as his hands squeezed the rag in his palms.

"Can I help you?"

"Are you Kazmierski?"

"Yes."

"Tyler Kazmierski?"

"My son."

The skinny man turned his head and nodded to the large one.

The big guy shifted on his feet. "When was the last time you spoke to Tyler?"

Ed looked at the man. "Who are you?"

"It doesn't matter, when was the last time you spoke with Tyler?"

"Get out of my shop."

The man walked closer, and Ed watched as his companion locked the door and flipped the Open sign. He had seen enough movies to know what was coming next.

"I need you to think very carefully and I'm going to ask you one more time. Tyler . . . when did you last talk with him?"

Ed's veins went cold. The man's face was devoid of any emotion. He looked like an automaton bent on getting what it wanted with little regard for humanity.

"Years," Ed said. He could feel the crack in his voice and he hated himself for it.

"When?"

"Years. Last I heard from him was when he was in El Paso. In jail. Years ago."

"Nothing since then?"

"No," Ed said.

"No?" the man said as he stepped closer.

"I swear, nothing. For all I know he's dead," Ed said, and as soon as the words came out of his mouth, he felt like he had just compromised himself. A small grin crossed the man's face.

"Who knows, maybe he is," the man said and let out a forced laugh. He flicked his head toward the back room. "What's back there?"

Ed turned his gaze, but before he could respond to the question, the man's fist swung out, sending Ed stumbling back a step in surprise. Another fist landed on the side of his head and he dropped to the floor, the ceiling spinning in circles. It had happened so fast that, before Ed could make sense of what was happening, the large man by the door walked over, grabbed his feet, and dragged him to the back. The man cleared the workbench and lifted Ed, propping him against it.

"Don't move." The command was punctuated with a fist to Ed's abdomen. He doubled over. The man grabbed Ed's hand and placed it on the bench. He grabbed a long screwdriver and held it over Ed's shaking limb, preparing to stake his hand to the table.

Ed had no idea the amount of pain that was coming next.

The bell over the front door rang and the world stopped around them. The tool held by the large man hovered over Ed's fingers, its momentum suspended in time. The tall man stared wide-eyed at both of them as they heard the front door close and a voice.

"Ed? You here?"

It was Tom.

Good old Tom. One of the last of the old-school cops who had a key ring with every store owner in Jennison's key attached to it, because who didn't trust Tom to check on the security of their investments.

"Ed?"

The tall man pulled a pistol out of his coat and slowly inched toward the door that led to the front. He pressed against the wall, waiting for the interloper to breach the opening. The large man pulled Ed to his feet and slapped his meaty paw over his mouth. His other hand produced a long serrated blade that almost instantly found the edge of Ed's neck. He pulled Ed farther back into the shadows of the room.

They could hear Tom slowly walking up the aisle of the shop, a faint whistle on his breath.

"Ed, you back there?"

The tall man slowly extended his arm, the pistol held out, at the ready to fire at whatever came through the door. The gunman's thumb moved onto the hammer. Ed could see the cylinder slowly turn as the weapon was cocked without a sound. Tom was just two more steps away from a bullet entering his left temple. His concern for the citizens of Jennison would be his end.

Then, as if by a miracle, the silence was shattered by radio chatter.

"Tom," the static voice said, "we got an accident over on Lincoln and Newberg."

The sound of a walkie-talkie being pulled from a leather belt and the click of the receiver.

"Anybody hurt?"

"Doesn't seem like it. Ambulance is on its way over just because."

"Alright, I'll be right there."

The sound of retreating steps echoed through the store, followed by the opening of the door, the ringing of the bell, and the noise of Tom locking the door again.

A collective breath exhaled in the back room. Ed saw the tall man uncock the gun and put it back in his shoulder holster. The knife came away from Ed's throat, and the large man pushed him away.

Ed was convinced that his heart had stopped beating five minutes ago and he tried to take a deep breath. He couldn't focus, as the adrenaline in his system was not letting him process what was happening. Relief came from an unlikely place. A fist hit him in the temple and he slumped down, unable to tell if he was blacking out or dying, but by the time his head hit the ground, Ed had surrendered to unconsciousness.

14

Roberto and Miguel found themselves in a caravan heading south to the airfield, Roberto knuckling the steering wheel, his nerves constricting at the thought that this was just a ruse. That as soon as they arrived, Salazar's men would gather around and execute him, and probably Miguel too. The boss would use him as an example of what happens when someone doesn't follow orders, doesn't do the job.

Roberto wasn't in with the Cartel. He was part of Los Diablos, a gang of poor Mexicans bound by ethnic locality. They were the enforcers for Salazar and his industry. Subcontractors who collected, intimidated, or murdered. It kept the boss's organization clean. The Cartel was brutal in execution, they had no qualms about killing anybody who got in their way, but they had the money, money that every kid on the border wanted a piece of, and so they found that it was little cost to "hire" these gangs and thugs to do some dirty work.

It seemed to work, right up to the point when it didn't. The Zetas had been trained by the US military to crack down on the drug trade in Mexico. But the money was too good, so they flipped the script and sold their services to the Gulf Cartel. As brutal as they were, they figured they might as well get rid of the Gulf Cartel and take over themselves.

The carnage was unprecedented.

Now, every *capo* was on alert to the ambitions of their paid enforcers. If Salazar knew that Roberto had not followed through executing Tyler, he was a dead man walking. He was so sure that this drive would be his last.

The airfield came into view and the train of vehicles pulled off the road and parked sporadically on the hardpan, dust rising all about them. Roberto stopped the car and Miguel woke up.

"We here?"

"Yes."

Miguel opened the door, stepped out, and walked toward the assembling crowd of people. Roberto took a deep breath and did the same.

Was this his last walk?

He wasn't afraid of death. Death hung around him like a cloud, and Lord knew he had dealt out his fair share of it. But it was always quick. He figured that when his time would come, it would be in a barrage of gunfire, a drive-by, or a nighttime assassination. But this long agonizing anticipation amplified the fear in his guts. He had seen others during this time, shaking and crying, begging for mercy, defecating and wetting themselves, crying to Mary or their mothers. Then the slow painful infliction of blows and cuts and acts that were only dreamed up in the depraved minds of men who had grown bored with simple killing.

He did not want that. He would not have that.

He felt for the gun in his waistband. He would empty the clip before they took him. Or . . . he would use it against himself and save himself from the humiliation of a slow death.

He walked up to the group and stood at the end of the line. Small talk among low-level thugs filled the still desert air.

A car arrived, its black exterior coated with grime from the drive, its darkened windows masking the people inside. It pulled closer to the landing strip and sat there idling. No one got out. Roberto watched in anticipation, his fingers on the cool steel on his back. He watched the others for any sudden movement.

And then, he heard it.

South, toward a distant hill rise, the sound of a plane coming in low. It materialized out of the sky and buzzed the airfield low, banked a wide arc, then came in for a landing. The aircraft taxied up the strip and stopped fifty meters from the car. Its door opened and a ladder was extended. Several men started to deboard the plane, and Roberto saw the same activity happening with the late-arriving car. He saw Salazar emerge from the vehicle and make his way to the newly arrived contingent. They all shook hands, and one of the men, a tall well-dressed individual, walked toward the shaded chairs with Salazar.

Roberto dropped his hands and he could feel the tension slowly draining from his shoulders.

So, this was legit. They were only here as a show of power for this clandestine meeting. The muscle that the politician brought with him huddled close to the plane while Salazar's goons stood solemnly near the road. Whatever the two men were talking about was their business.

After thirty minutes, the activity followed

a reverse order, and Roberto and Miguel were in their car driving back to Nuevo Negaldo. They didn't talk. They simply drove, and Roberto knew he had a little more time to clean up the mess he had made and get Tyler out of his life forever.

15

The world slowly came back to him and Ed strained to see clearly. The ceiling of his workroom began to stabilize at the same speed as the pain in his head increased. Fully conscious, his skull throbbed. He got to his feet and made his way to the store-front. The place was empty. He went to the door, opened it, and looked outside. It felt like any afternoon in Jennison. A school bus was heading east down Main.

Ed went back inside and called Tom.

"What happened to you?" Tom said as he walked in.

"Got jumped by a couple of guys."

"You know who?"

"No."

"What did they want?"

"Take a guess."

Ed could tell that Tom would have guessed right if he had been the kind of man to say anything bad about another's offspring.

"You need me to get you to a doctor?"

"No, but I was wondering if you wouldn't mind going out to the house with me."

"You think they might be out there?"

"I don't know. I just would like some backup if they are."

"Sure thing," Tom said.

Ed gathered his things and soon the two were in a mini convoy out to Ed's house. Tom took the lead and pulled up closest to the house, parking so as to use the car as a shield, depending on what they might find. Ed pulled up behind.

The front door was open, the screen knocked off its hinges. From his vantage point, Ed could tell there were pieces of his life tossed to the floor, ransacked, parts blowing in the wind off the porch and into the fields.

Tom reached into his car and pushed down on the horn. It shrieked in the still air. They waited but saw no movement coming from inside. Ed watched as Tom unholstered his weapon and approached the porch. Ed started behind him. Tom turned and motioned Ed toward the police car and made a pumping motion with his hands. Inside the car was a shotgun. Ed retrieved it and came up behind him.

They entered the house, and slowly went

from room to room. Up the stairs, step by step, Ed could feel his stomach tightening. He had never been in a fight, never been close to being shot at, and within the past several hours that omission in his history was now filled.

The two men swept the house, but it was empty. Whoever the men were, they were long gone.

"What do you think they were looking for?"

"Tyler," Ed said, deflated. "But I told them the same thing I told the agent on the phone, I haven't seen him for years."

"Well, wherever he is, he sure has stirred up some trouble."

The sheriff asked more questions about the incident, told Ed he would get on the horn with state police and see if they could find the perpetrators, though Ed figured they were halfway back to Mexico by now.

"You want me to help you clean up a bit?"

"No, I'll take care of it," Ed said as he walked out to the porch, picked up the upturned chair, and took a seat.

"You sure?"

"Yeah. Go on home. Thanks for coming out here with me."

Tom went back into the house. Ed could hear him opening the refrigerator and pulling a bottle out. The sheriff reappeared and handed a bottle of beer over, then placed his shotgun against the railing next to Ed.

"Those guys come back" — Tom nodded at the gun — "just shoot 'em first." He headed for his car.

"Hey, Tom?"

"Yeah?"

"I'm going to head out tomorrow, go down and see what this might be about. You mind watching over my place until I get back?"

"No problem. Just take care of yourself."

Ed nodded and watched as the sheriff left. Ed sipped his beer and the resolve in his gut quickened. If they came back, they would not find him here. He would be on his way to Nuevo Negaldo.

16

A single beam of sunlight arched across the interior of a one-room apartment several hours north of Mexico City.

Two men occupied this space today. One was rinsing a razor in a bowl of water. The other was seated, blindfolded, his hands bound behind his back.

El Matacerdos slowly shaved the face of the man tied in the chair. He carefully worked his way around the throat and chin, below the nose, despite the heavy breathing of the blindfolded man. El Matacerdos knew by now that his captive would not attempt to talk, to yell out, once having the duct tape removed from his mouth. They had been over this several times the past two weeks.

"I am not your judge, I am not your confessor," El Matacerdos said the first night after he was required to beat the man into silence. It only took three more days for the hostage to understand that it was no use to plead, beg, or scream. El Matacerdos was not a man you could bargain with.

El Matacerdos had orders and they came from his cell phone. Only one person had the number. The highest member of the Cartel. This was the voice of the Cartel's angel of death.

He did not create the script but merely played his role as it was passed down to him. His phone would ring, he would listen, he would confirm, and he would execute. Whatever the order. His current assignment consisted of sitting in this room with the hostage. Sometimes he was told to remove a piece . . . a finger, a toe. Other times it was simply a beating. The last call was an hour ago. It was to make the man presentable.

El Matacerdos had washed the hostage and was now finishing up the shave. The swelling in the man's face was subsiding, though the coloring would take much longer to heal. The shaving now complete, El Matacerdos reapplied the tape to the man's mouth.

The chore done, he sat down in front of the television. The images rolled by, but he might as well have been watching static, as none of it registered in his consciousness.

He did not daydream, he merely existed. Robotic. Lost in his own world of vast open space.

The streak of sunlight moved across the room as time passed.

The prisoner in the chair began to cough, the air trapped in his throat, pushing against the tape. El Matacerdos stood, walked over, removed the tape, and held a glass of water to the man's lips. The man drank at it dog-like, but was able to swallow a few ounces and subside his spasm. The tape went back on.

The motes danced in the sunlight.

The cell phone rang.

Muffled words through an earpiece.

"Yes," El Matacerdos replied.

He put the phone in his pocket and stepped back behind the man in the chair. From his waistband he pulled out his 9mm, aimed, and shot the prisoner in the back of the head. The hostage slumped down as his lifeblood flowed from his head onto the floor.

El Matacerdos set the pistol on a table as he gathered up his things and stuffed them into a duffel bag. He washed his hands in the sink, turned off the TV, and left the room. As he walked down the hall toward the stairwell, a door cracked open and an old woman's eye appeared. He looked at her and she slammed the door. He made his way down the stairs, out to the parking lot, and got into his car.

As he drove away, his eyes grew heavy focusing on the stretch of road before him. He would drive north, closer to where his soul was, and wait for the next set of orders to be given to him. But for now he was again his own man, and his thoughts went blank as he lost himself in a song on the radio.

17

Ed stood in front of his bathroom mirror. The bruising on the right side of his face was starting to purple where he had been punched. On his neck he could feel the abrasion from the knife blade that had been pressed against his throat. The whole time-line of the events that he had experienced blurred together. In the past forty-eight hours, he had received a call from a stranger in New Mexico with a cryptic message about his son, was contacted by a federal officer about a drug ring that Tyler was caught up with, as well as being jumped in his shop by two thugs looking for the same answers that Agent Lomas was seeking.

How had life flipped upside down in so short a time?

Ed soaked a towel in cold water, pressed it against his temple, and held it there. He had never taken a shot like this before. Part of him felt a little tougher having endured it, like he had earned something by the physical assault and walked away. His nerves were rattled, but it also served to coalesce his determination to go south.

He walked to the overturned bookcase in his bedroom and from the pile of books on the floor pulled out an old road atlas that hadn't been used since, well, since how long? Since the trip to Denver. The trip that the stranger had mentioned in the phone call.

He carried the atlas into the kitchen and laid it on the table. As if by design, it opened on Colorado and there before him, marked in a black pen, was the history of the trip that he and Tyler had taken after his wife left for California. Looking for a way to console the boy over the reality of being abandoned, and also wanting to escape the house that all of a sudden felt hollow, the two had set off on a road trip west to an amusement park. It was the first time that father and son had ever really done anything on their own. Come to think of it, Ed thought, it might have been the only time.

He flipped the pages over to New Mexico and, with his finger, traced the southern border of the picture until he found the border town of Nuevo Negaldo. It appeared to be a couple hours west of El Paso with no major highway going directly to it. Just what appeared to be county roads. There was nothing around it, just some topographic lines of hills, or valleys or mountains, Ed didn't know which.

Going back and forth, he figured out the route he would need to take to get there, and guessed at how long. Twelve hours? Maybe longer?

With a pen he charted a course on the map, the dark line terminating at the small dot on the Mexico border. He pulled out the scrap of paper he'd slid into his pocket and glanced at it.

Plaza Motel
La Casa de Irma
Ask for Ibanez

Ed went to his bedroom closet, found an old duffel bag, and put some clothes in it. He set it at the foot of his bed and lay down, the pain in his head resurfacing with the sudden burst of activity.

Was he actually going to go?

His life went on without his son just fine. In fact, he found that he hardly ever thought of where he might be, the same as he never thought where his ex-wife had ended up. He had just . . . moved on. Done his own thing. Let people go their way while he went his. Sometimes an acquaintance would ask about Tyler, and he would give a vague answer, and at that point feel a twinge of something in his soul that bordered on guilt of not knowing where in the world his son was, but it would pass just as easily as a light breeze on a calm day.

But now it was as if he was forced back into considering his progeny.

And what would he find there? And what, if anything, could his getting involved do to sort out this mess which seemed as violent and corrupt as his imagination could fathom?

All these thoughts swirled in his head and were ultimately repelled by the growing conviction that he just had to go. He could call Agent Lomas, but again, his gut, which had always served him well, hinted that that was not the right course of action.

No, tomorrow morning he would go at least to the border. He would go see this Ibanez at La Casa de Irma.

He would allow himself at least a look into the mystery before turning his back on Tyler again.

18

"Your father."

Those words, no matter how old the man, will always cause a son's heart to pause.

Tyler remained on his cot in the cell below the church. He slept, woke and vomited, passed out, woke again, tried to stand, fell back down, and repeated the process over and over. His wound felt like lead, his stomach was raw from the antibiotics, his body was restless from lying prone, his head ached from lack of calories.

But what brought the most pain to his mind were those words.

"Your father."

This sick man's tomb he was in felt like a magnified version of the principal's office, the sheriff's cruiser, the holding cell at the local jail. His whole life flashed before him like a looped script where he was waiting for his father to show up. And that waiting would grind the nerves of his body until he saw his dad and the disappointment and coldness he brought with him.

His dad had never done much of anything when he arrived, so it was irrational to worry. Perhaps it is written in a boy's biology to fear the wrath of his father. The anticipation of its arrival far exceeding the action meted out.

Tyler's dad wasn't much for words.

He wasn't much for anything.

When his mom had left, his dad had pretty much shut down. He provided the mechanical duties of home life — food, shelter, clothing. When it came to emotions, communication, that was all but lost.

Why, then, when the priest said that his father was being contacted, did it make his heart drop?

It didn't make sense.

After all these years not hearing from him, what made him flush with anxiety, Tyler realized, was knowing that he wouldn't show up. That he was alone in the world, and as Felipe intimated, there wasn't anybody else in the world who would vouch for him. Who would come to his aid.

Tyler was scared.

And what he was scared of was finding out that in this, his most desperate hour, the most desperate he had ever been in, his

father wouldn't show up.
That was his fear.
That was his pain.

19

Ed was up and on the road by seven the next morning.

His eye still felt two sizes too big and the bruising on his face had gotten more pronounced overnight, but he downed several aspirin with his morning coffee. He had grabbed his things, locked up the disheveled house, and headed out.

Kansas blurred into Oklahoma and in turn melted into Texas. The high prairie grass extended in every direction with the occasional black smudge of a cattle herd breaking the monotony. The air was crisp and the sky clear. It would be a rather unexciting trip as far as driving was concerned, which was fine with Ed, as his mind was bending to the point of breaking, thinking about what he was driving toward.

Fifty years down in his life and all had been quiet compared to the past two days. His life wasn't a novel. It was just his, and all of a sudden he had been pushed into a story line that seemed as far from his life as any movie that might have been showing in town.

The radio passed the time for most of the morning, but soon the sounds became more of an irritant on his ever-quickening nerves. He shut it off and let his own thoughts fill the gap.

Tyler.

He remembered the day his son was born like it had happened yesterday. Sitting in the delivery room, his hands shaking as they lifted the boy over the partition into his wife's arms. He was in awe and had no words to express the feeling that was going through his body. That moment in time where all things are possible, a new life with no past and an unwritten future. It was like pulling a new book off the shelf and cracking the spine for the first time, not knowing where the tale will take you. But somewhere along the path, the romance turned to tragedy and the tome was placed back on the shelf, the reader no longer interested in how the tale would end.

He drove on.

As he went south, the world seemed to stretch out, the trees along the road grew bush-like, and the blue sky unfolded in an endless horizon.

He had worked, his wife raised Tyler — until she got tired of being a simple utility in other people's lives and took off for glory. Maybe he wouldn't have tried to stop her, knowing that she had checked out long before the day she left. Afterward, he simply worked more that day and arrived home late, Tyler in front of the TV, and cold cuts for dinner. The two didn't talk much about it, but he did remember hearing his son crying himself to sleep over the next couple of months.

Ed didn't know what a child needed. He had convinced himself he didn't have a clue.

He drove on, the next mile looking like the fifty before.

The world was flat, as if his thoughts would roll forever on a continuous horizontal plane.

He should have gone into Tyler's room. Should have taken his boy up in his arms and let him bury his tears in his chest. That's what he should have done. But he hadn't. He had simply sat in the living room, the TV glow illuminating the dark house, the silent cries of a wounded boy filtering down the stairs. Ed didn't know how to fix this. He didn't know what to do and so he did nothing in the hopes that some solution would materialize to take away the boy's pain.

But nothing ever had.

20

Camilla made her way through the kitchen, cleaning up the mess from the day before at the same time that she was getting herself ready and presentable. She did her hair, a bit of makeup, dressed, ate, and started packing her bag. The curiosity and anxiety of the past two days had lost their edge. The phone call to the stranger two days ago was followed by a completely uneventful yesterday.

When she rolled in just before midnight, Roberto was not at home.

She was tired and went straight to bed. At one point in the middle of the night, she heard him come in and crash in his own room.

As she finished up her morning routine and prepared to leave for work, she opened up Roberto's door and looked inside. He lay on his side, facing the wall, a sheet half covering his body. He had slept in his clothes, his shoes still on his feet.

She walked over quietly to him and bent down to kiss his head.

The movement of her breath or the sounds of her steps woke him and Roberto darted up, his body pushing itself into the wall like a wild animal cornered by a predator. His right arm was outstretched and his gun was pointed right at her. In his eyes was panic, fear, sleep. Camilla screamed and fell to the floor.

"Roberto! Roberto! It's me!" she yelled.

Her son's gaze darted across the room, the gun chasing ghosts that raced before his open eyes. His breath was shallow and rapid and he slowly came back to reality.

"Mama?"

"It's me, Roberto!"

Roberto lowered the gun and sank back down on the bed. Camilla raised her head, tears in the corners of her eyes. He looked at her, threw the pistol down, stepped off the bed, and tried to comfort her.

She muffled her cries in her throat. She knew who he was when she wasn't looking, but the sight of her boy as a *pistolero* crushed her.

"Mama . . . Mama, I'm sorry. You hear me? I'm sorry," he said, squeezing her.

Camilla slowly composed herself. "What

is going on, Roberto? What is happening?"

"Nothing."

"Don't tell me nothing," she said, standing and pushing him away. Her fear morphed into anger with the speed that only a mother possesses. She wiped her eyes and stared at her son still kneeling on the floor in front of her. "Why do you have that gun? In my house? Tell me! What is going on."

"Nothing, Mama. Just go to work. It's fine."

"It's not fine, Roberto. What have you gotten yourself into?"

He didn't say anything but stood, moved the sheets until he found the gun, and put it in his waistband. He turned and looked at her.

"Who was that man you had me call?"

He sat on the bed and motioned for her to do the same. He told the story, leaving out the parts about himself that would solidify her thoughts about his descent into violence.

"He is the one from El Paso? The one you said helped you out in jail?"

"Yes."

Camilla let out a long breath. "And he's with Felipe now?"

"Yes."

Another breath. She stood, gathered up

her things, and straightened herself. "And what if he doesn't come, Tyler's father? What happens to him then?"

"I don't know."

"Are they going to come after you? Do they know it was you who hid him with Felipe?"

Roberto looked at her and said nothing but simply walked past her and into the kitchen. There was a knock on the front door and both mother and son froze still.

"Roberto! Are you in there?"

It was Miguel.

Roberto went to the door and opened it. The sunshine flooded the house and a large shadow in the shape of Miguel's massive frame fell on Camilla.

"Come on, let's go," Miguel said.

Roberto turned, gave his mother a kiss on the cheek. "Go to work, Mama. Don't worry about me. Everything is going to be fine. There is nothing for you to worry about."

She watched him go. But the worry he told her not to suffer poured into her heart, and she sent up a silent prayer in the empty house.

21

"Remember Denver."

At the end of one summer, the year that his wife had left, Edward and Tyler had loaded up the truck and driven to Denver. He had forgotten about that trip until the phone call.

The amusement park was a distraction. Thrill rides giving the pair five-minute reprieves from the repressed feelings they were both keeping bottled up. Late that night, as the park was closing, they had gotten separated. The crowds started thinning out until the only people left were the maintenance and security crews walking between the rides. Ed could not find his son.

Panic started welling up inside of him as he went from attraction to attraction, asking if anyone had seen his boy, but no one had. Ed could hear Tyler's name being broadcast on the walkie-talkies as he ran, yelling out in his own voice. Twenty minutes later, he saw Tyler sitting on a bench next to a security guard. He ran to him, scooped him up, and held him tight.

Ed found that he was crying, and so was Tyler.

They left the park without saying much, but with a common understanding that they would not abandon each other as his wife had done.

Unfortunately, emotions spurred by desperation don't linger long after the adrenaline subsides. Thinking now of the moment, that twenty minutes of panic, Ed could recall the feeling of that night. He realized he hadn't felt that way in a very long time.

It slowly dawned on him that that was why he was driving down to New Mexico.

It wasn't the mystery. It wasn't anger toward the two thugs who came close to maiming him at his shop. The men who had ransacked his house. It was the memory of that feeling.

"Remember Denver."

That was why he was driving. The heart moves faster than the mind, even for a man who thinks himself made of stone.

A ten-hour car trip alone is as good as any psychotherapy that can be bought.

He was driving to Nuevo Negaldo because his son was lost and needed his dad. What else could that line have meant? Who else but Tyler could have said it? After all these years, a simple phrase had pricked his conscience and awoken him to his duty.

And thus he drove to whatever he would find.

The country was dotted with scrapyards surrounded by aluminum fencing, filled with cars from previous travelers of histories past. Abandoned homesteads where people had tried to put down roots, thought better of it, and moved on. Cacti freckled the yellow plain as far as the eye could see, sotol plants shooting their stems into the sky like spears.

By late afternoon he drove into El Paso. A river of concrete and steel flowed from the south and broke against the Franklin Mountains. Somewhere the border cut through the sea of buildings. He filled up on gas and some food, found the border road into New Mexico, and drove west.

It felt as if he had left the world of man behind him as he continued on into the borderlands. The road was pristine blacktop devoid of any sign of civilization, as if the asphalt was laid down just to prove that man was greater than nature and not for any realistic utility. To his left he could occasionally see the vehicle barrier running beside him that provided the only indication as to where the US ended and Mexico began.

The miles went on.

He passed by several border patrol vehicles parked in the scrub and pullouts. He checked his rearview to see if they would follow, but they never did.

He checked the clock, the miles, his gas gauge, and kept driving.

As the sun started skirting the western hills, he thought he saw some signs of life up ahead and came to a crossroads. There was a single-pump gas station and he pulled in to top off his tank. He went inside and grabbed some snacks, handed some cash to the old Mexican behind the till, then asked how far it was to Hurtado.

"Eh?" the man said.

"Hurtado . . . how far to Hurtado?"

"Hurtado? Hour."

"An hour?"

The man nodded and handed back change.

Ed went back to his truck, got in the cab, and opened the atlas. He traced his route and found where he was. Another twenty minutes west and then he would have to turn south. He assumed that it would be the next road he came to. It was getting dark and he very well could miss it, so he took off at a more urgent speed.

He found the road, turned south, and after what seemed like too long finally caught sight of some distant lights. He saw a sign that said HURTADO, 3 MILES, as well as a warning that a border checkpoint was coming up. He arrived and his cramped legs and back almost jumped for joy.

There wasn't much to show for Hurtado, New Mexico. Several trailers and cinder-block homes were laid out on dirt street grids to one side of the north-south road. On the eastern side was a building that looked like an old train depot for a rail service that had disappeared a century ago. Several cars were in the parking lot, and a lighted sign hung from a rusted pole that said La Casa de Irma. He slowly drove past it, and on his right he saw the Plaza Motel.

Ed pulled in, went inside, and got a room from an attendant who was surprised to have another visitor. He went to his room, used the bathroom to freshen up, and then walked over to the restaurant in hopes that the mysterious voice that went by the name Ibanez was there.

22

Ed walked into La Casa de Irma and looked around. There were a couple people scattered about, finishing up meals and drinks and conversations. It had the appearance of closing time, but a voice called out to him from the kitchen to have a seat and help would be on the way. He went to an empty table close to the door and sat down. He fiddled with the condiments in the chrome centerpiece as he waited.

A woman approached who walked as if she had been standing all day. She was dark and attractive, and when she smiled, her eyes disappeared behind thick lashes.

"Can I get you something to drink?" she asked.

"Beer, whatever you have," Ed said.

"Anything to eat?"

Her voice sounded exotic to his midwestern ears. Perhaps it was the exhaustion of the long drive, the adrenaline depletion of the past twenty-four hours, or the fact that he was still a man, middle-aged as he was, but still a man, but the woman before him captivated him like a dream. He picked up the menu and refocused himself, ordered a sandwich, and she walked away.

When she returned with his food, he asked her the question that he had driven hundreds of miles to ask.

"I'm looking for Ibanez?"

The waitress's eyes widened for a brief moment, then looked around at the other tables to make sure that everyone was minding their own business. The woman opened her mouth to speak but then turned on her heels and darted for the kitchen. Ed watched her go and sat staring at the door that the waitress ran through. He didn't know what might emerge from that opening and he braced himself. But the woman returned, appearing a bit more composed than when she left. She looked at Ed and quietly spoke.

"I am she. I am Camilla Ibanez."

"You the one who called me?"

"Yes."

Camilla stared at Ed, examining him, her face tired yet youthful. They seemed caught up in a moment of silence that neither knew how to get out of. Ed had followed her instructions, but she apparently had no more to give.

"Well, I'm here," Ed said.

Ed could tell she was sizing him up. "Yes. I was just expecting . . ."

"What?"

"I'm not sure. Usually the people my Roberto deals with do not look like you."

"Like me?"

"Middle-aged white guys with bruised faces."

"Oh." Ed didn't know what to say.

"I just . . . well, I heard Tyler was gringo, but I still was not expecting . . ."

"You know Tyler?"

"Yes. Well, no. I have heard about him. Roberto has talked about him."

"Roberto?"

"My son."

Ed stared up at Camilla. He waited for her to continue. But nothing more was said.

"So what now?"

"I'll let Roberto know you came."

"And then?"

"I have no idea," she said.

Ed studied her face. She was telling the truth. She had no idea what this was all about besides passing a message between people. She became aware that she was standing over his table for far too long and went over to assist the other patrons. He drank his beer, finished his sandwich, and left money for the bill. He stood and walked to the exit, catching her eye as he reached for the door. She gave him a look, one of both concern and comfort, a look of re-assurance that she would bring him more information soon.

He walked into the night, across the empty desert street, and back to his room at the Plaza Motel.

23

Camilla closed up the restaurant, got in her car, and drove south toward the border checkpoint. She passed the Plaza Motel and tried to figure out which of the three vehicles parked out front was Edward Kazmierski's.

A couple miles down the road, the lights of the border crossing illuminated the interior of her car and she passed without incident. She drove down Revolución Street, the city calm as if holding its breath. She arrived home, parked her car in the rock drive, and made her way inside. The world was dark and she could hear the music of a cantina several blocks away, but her street was quiet with the silence of decent people locked behind closed doors.

Once inside, she turned on the small lamp in the corner, which revealed a small open space bordered by a tiny kitchen. There was a couch, and a television, with bedding stacked neatly against the wall.

She was never sure if Roberto would be there, his body sprawled out on the old piece of furniture, but in her heart she always hoped that he would. Better to be here than *out there* doing the things that she knew he did but did not ask him about.

She placed her bag on the floor, took the dinner she had brought with her from work into the kitchen, and prepared a plate. The dim light shone across the space and illuminated her face. She prayed for blessing, crossed herself, and began to eat.

Soon she heard steps coming toward the front door. They were slow, as if the person had been working all day in the heat and each step up was done out of sheer force of will. The person turned the handle and opened the door.

Roberto.

He came inside, closed the door quickly, and locked it. He parted the curtain, looked out into the street, and backed away from the door. She watched as he stood there, a tremor in his body as if he was waiting for the devil to come charging through the door.

"Roberto," Camilla said with a stern voice.

He jumped and turned on her, his cold stare softening when his eyes met hers. His posture softened and he came over to give her a kiss on the cheek.

"Hello, Mama," he said.

"I have food for you."

"I'm not hungry."

She ignored him and handed him a plate.

"Sit down, here."

He complied.

"He came today," she said.

Roberto froze. The anxiety on his face looked about ready to break his jaw. The utensil in his hand hit against the plate.

"He did?"

"*Sí.*"

"What did he look like?"

"Like any other gringo. Out of place."

"That's not what I mean, Mama. Did he look like he will go? Go to Felipe?"

"I don't know. But he came this far. That is a good thing, right?"

Roberto nodded. The tension in his body was palpable. Camilla stood and put her arms around her son. She felt his shoulders soften as he relaxed in his mother's embrace.

"Alright," he whispered as he stood and started pacing. His mother watched him. "Alright . . ."

She waited, giving him space, which he appreciated. His own voice in his head couldn't handle another speaker.

"Do you know where he is?"

"Yes, he is staying at the motel in Hurtado."

"Will you give him a message?"

"Yes."

"Good. Tell him to meet Felipe at two at La Terraza."

"I will."

Roberto looked around the room. They had lived here his whole life. This small apartment was his childhood, his existence. His mind raced to what would happen if they ever found out he had betrayed them. What they would do to his mama. Their lives splattered against the walls and floors.

It had been a stupid play. He should have just killed Tyler. What was he to him anyway? Why had he felt so duty bound? But now he was here, with his mama, envisioning their own execution if Tyler's father would not go and take his son back home, away from the eyes of the Cartel.

Roberto's pulse was racing when he felt his mother's hand on his back.

"Son . . . ," she whispered.

He turned. She saw the worry in his eyes.

"I am proud of you."

"Why, Mama. What could you be proud of?"

"For trying," she said. "For trying, at last, to do the right thing."

"I'm not sure I did the right thing."

She hugged him and could feel the fear coursing through his body. She held him, remembering the times when he was little, before all his bad decisions had led him to places she never dreamed he would go in her worst nightmares. "I believe you did. Trust that you did."

He stepped back and looked at her. "Did he look like he would help?" he asked again, looking for any sign of hope.

"You can't control that. You can only keep trying to do the right things."

"I think it's too late for me. This might be the only time."

"Don't say that, Roberto."

"The world doesn't reward doing right, Mama. You know that."

She looked at him. She had had him for a moment, and then he was gone again.

24

What did he know of Mexico?

Nothing.

Ed looked out the window of the motel room, down on the paper map of Nuevo Negaldo that he held in his hand, and back outside. The sun high, reflecting off the steel roofs and cars, illuminated the otherwise empty desert landscape. To his eyes, the road south looked like one long concrete serpent slithering between jagged terrain. But somewhere down there, a line was drawn. A border.

He strained a bit and thought he could make out a fence, a wall, some demarcation line, but more or less it was his imagination filling in the blanks of a wide-open horizon.

Here on the US side, he felt at ease, but when his thoughts drifted to Nuevo Negaldo, he could feel the tension in his chest.

What did he know of Mexico?

Camilla Ibanez had slipped the envelope under his door that morning. He watched as she crossed over the road to the restaurant and disappeared inside. In the envelope was a note saying to meet a man named Felipe at a place called La Terraza. There was a map with a circle around the location. On paper, it looked innocuous. In his imagination, he was journeying into a war zone.

Ed and his wife had vacationed in Cancún one year after saving up for an excessively long period. He would say that he had been to Mexico when people asked him, but it was as authentic and all-encompassing a response as if a traveler visiting New York City said they saw America.

Growing up, he had worked a summer in the fields with the migrant workers who came up from Sinaloa by the truckload. They had kept to themselves, a mysterious band of laborers. They worked hard and then drove south when the fields were harvested. Ed never went back, taking next summer's work at a warehouse in Wichita that was air-conditioned. He often wondered if those same caravans went back to the same fields. Were they there now, all these years later?

What did he know of Mexico?

Just stories.

Singular, well-placed stories.

Ed heard of the drug war, the Cartels, the killings, the violence. Nuevo Negaldo was one of several border cities hemorrhaging bodies every day. However, as he looked south toward the mystery of a strange land, it was impossible to believe that everyone in Mexico was complicit in atrocities. The lights from Nuevo Negaldo hinted at a city that was alive with noise and movement. Of restaurants and bars, music and parks and shopping. Mexicans were not just migrants or Cartel sicarios, just as Ed was an American but not an ignorant imperialist.

But why was he afraid? Why did gazing south of the border fill him with apprehension?

The sounds around him, even though he was on US soil in Hurtado, were as foreign to him as if he had landed on the moon. The dry smell of the high desert, the language filling his ears as he walked back from the motel to the restaurant again, was anxiety inducing. He was the minority. He was the outsider, and for Ed, this was not his usual view on the world.

He knew that once he crossed the border, he would be a sitting duck. Unable to speak Spanish, unable to navigate apart from the printed-out map of the location. A wrong turn would put him into the bowels of Nuevo Negaldo with no way to ask for help. And who would he ask? The police?

He had heard stories.

But was it *all* the police? Or were the stories extrapolated from single anecdotes to paint with a wide brush?

The notion of standing on a street corner with a paper map in hand, trying to decipher where to go, would be like putting a sign around his neck that said "Rob Me Please." He looked down at the map again. He was doing his best to memorize it: across the border checkpoint, five blocks south, turn right, three blocks west, zig this way and then that. He tried to remember the back-street names, but the string of consonants and vowels were run together in a way that his memory could not record them.

Standing here contemplating his journey, the only thing he knew of Mexico was that it made him afraid.

25

Ed walked out of Hurtado, south down the two-lane road toward the border crossing. It was a tin carport enclosure buttressed on both sides by the tall border wall. Cars were backed up single file coming north, passing through the scrutiny of US customs and the prying noses of a K9 unit. The path into Mexico was clear, as if he was the only one on earth that morning with an interest on the other side of the border.

As he walked, he felt the nerves start to grip his stomach. West on the horizon, out past the two cities, the land would have looked unchanged for miles upon miles, had it not been for the high metal wall. This artificial barrier in the wilderness. He was about to cross over into a world so foreign that every cell in his body told him to stop.

He kept walking.

Nuevo Negaldo, the Mexican sister city to Hurtado, washed up right against the wall, its stucco and brick buildings appearing as debris swept up in an ocean of desert and deposited against the steel structure. He could not read the signs.

Ed walked under the tin awning, followed the sidewalk, and before he knew it, he was on Mexican soil. Two army soldiers leaned against a railing, their automatic weapons slung against their green fatigues, talking to each other. Neither one seemed to give him any notice. Ed kept walking until the checkpoint was behind him. He continued down the sidewalk, past the northbound traffic jam.

The doors to cantinas and trinket shops were open. Peering inside, Ed saw empty cement rooms with random plastic chairs, wooden bars filled with sweating bottles, and locals preparing for whatever customers might come in that day.

A mangy dog slept on its side in front of him, didn't move as Ed stepped over it, uninterested in an American venturing down the street.

Ed counted down the cross streets until he got to five, and then turned right. He kept his eyes from wandering too much and did his best to walk with purpose. With confidence. As if he belonged there. He felt as if eyes in the shadowed recesses of open doors were tracking his movements.

He kept walking until he saw, in the narrow corridor of an alleyway, a dilapidated sign over a doorway. Without breaking stride, he crossed the cement roadway, his nerves humming, and stepped inside.

Too many bad movies had filled Ed's mind on what to expect as he passed through the door and felt the cool air of shade lap over him. The barkeep was moving boxes in and out of a back room, while two men sat in chairs at the end of the bar. None appeared interested in his sudden appearance. Ed looked around before walking up to the bar, making sure there wasn't an unseen figure, someone waiting to kick him out into the street for being an American in the wrong place. But despite his overactive nerves, it became apparent to him that he could have robbed the place and no one would have noticed.

The slow realization of his own lack of importance started to comfort his anxiety. The bartender came back, grunted a sound accentuated in such a manner that Ed took it as a question.

"Beer, please?"

The man quickly fetched a bottle and set it down. Ed laid a five-dollar bill on the counter, which the man quickly scooped up and stuffed in his pocket. There would be no change given. Ed wouldn't know how to ask for it in Spanish anyway.

He walked over to an empty folding chair and card table near the door of the outer wall and sat down. He was able to gaze through the opening down the alley from which he had come. The sounds from the outside world disappeared — the line of cars moving slowly north, the beggars and window washers working the line for spare change, the yelling drivers who gave up some silver either out of charity or fear — all were muted as he sat in the hollow cool of the cantina.

He saw a dog in the street slowly rise to its feet, circle around, and then lie back down. At least it wasn't dead, Ed thought.

He suddenly felt extremely foolish. He had prepared himself for this short journey meticulously, gone over it again and again in his thoughts. His cell phone, his wallet, his keys, he had left them all in his room in Hurtado. Some loose bills and his passport were all he brought with him, so assured he was that he was going to be robbed, attacked, mugged. But the walk from the border to this shadowed table in a back-alley bar had been as uneventful as any weekend stroll in the park.

The worst stories are the only stories that climb over the wall. And it was the worst stories that filled Ed's knowledge of the border. The stories of bodies burned, decapitated heads left in the street, kidnappings, murders. That was all he had heard, and it came as a welcome surprise that he did not have to wade through blood to get to the rendezvous spot Camilla Ibanez had directed him to.

26

Ed sat at the corner table until his beer was empty. He went back for another, figuring alcohol was safer than water. He sat with his back against the wall and most of his body in shadow. The tavern was musty, as if the sweat of Pancho Villa still hung in the air after a hard day's ride.

Felipe wasn't showing up.

Time passed.

The second beer was nearly gone and the low buzz started filling his head. The knowledge of being an unwelcome guest was eating at his nerves. Being ignored by the three men in the establishment was just as unsettling. Ed could have had a heart attack and died in his chair and no one would bother to look after him for days. That, or a gunman would suddenly step through the door and put a bullet in his head. He didn't know which would happen, and both seemed a certainty.

A shadow graced the threshold of the cantina and a small man walked in. He had on a stained fabric overcoat which he wore comfortably even in the oppressive heat. Ed watched the man waddle to the bar, order a drink, and begin to scan the room. When his eyes alighted on Ed, his face softened and he walked over. He sat down and extended his hand.

"You must be Edward Kazmierski." His English was clear and only hinted at an accent. "I am Felipe."

Ed took his hand and shook it. When the man sat down, his coat opened, revealing for a brief moment a clerical collar around his neck.

"You're a priest?" Ed blurted out. The tone was one of surprised relief.

"Yes, even in this godless place, there is still a need for priests. Maybe now more than ever."

"Camilla didn't mention it."

"Camilla is cautious with information."

Ed took a sip of his beer and contemplated the man.

After settling in, Felipe brought his own glass to his lips and set it back down. "So, tell me why you are down here."

"I thought you were going to tell me."

"No, no, no. I don't know the *why*."

"Tyler. My son. Camilla called me saying that he was in trouble down here."

"Not the who. Why?"

"I guess to help him."

"Tell me about him."

"Not much to tell. I hardly know him myself." Ed shifted in his seat and stared back at the priest.

"In this day, my friend, that is not an impossible task."

"I kicked him out a long time ago."

"Perhaps that was the best thing for him?"

Ed thought about it. No, it was not the best thing for him, though it seemed so at the time. "What kind of dad does that? It's starting to eat at me."

"Even Peter denied the Son."

"Yeah," Ed said. He hid his reaction behind another sip from the bottle, using the pause to try to remember the story the priest was referring to. "I've been denying Tyler for well on six years."

"Yes, but the Gospel writers were very generous in only writing about that one night. Now, if they had written about all of Peter's days, well, perhaps he denied more, and just nobody heard it . . . eh?" The old priest cracked a smile.

"Perhaps."

"So you are here to soothe your conscience?"

"No."

"So why are you here?"

"To find out what's going on with Tyler."

"And?"

"And . . . I guess . . . help if I can."

"Good," Felipe said with a smile. "That is a noble thing. But now — now you need to ask yourself, are you here to save the memory, or to help the man? If you are here for your boy, then you are chasing at vapor, a mist of the mind. But to be here for the man means putting the memory of the boy to bed, and being willing to rescue that which he has become."

Ed took another slow drink. "Are you a priest or a philosopher?"

Felipe sat back in his chair, smiled, adjusted his collar, took in a deep breath, and started to speak of who he was.

27

You remember your son? Maybe when he was little? Yes? Running to you when he had a boo-boo on his knee? That boy is gone. He is not here in Nuevo Negaldo. He is not anywhere but between your ears. In your mind's eye. Perhaps you think that that memory is still in him, buried somewhere waiting to get out. In that case, you will leave here disappointed. In fact, best to leave now, go back north. Keep him in memory.

"To rescue that which you love requires sacrifice. I do not know your fate, amigo, but I do know that if you wish to save your son, then a sacrifice must be made. It may be something great that the Lord above has destined for you to lay down, or it may be something small. I do not know. But I do know that a sacrifice must be made. Maybe you will have to sacrifice that memory, those gentle times of his youth, to be able to look at him as the man he has turned out to be, or you may have to sacrifice the *man* in order to retain the memory of your sweet innocent boy."

Ed remained silent as Felipe paused, stretched his back, then continued.

"You look at me as if I'm crazy? Maybe so. One cannot live here without being partly crazy. But you and me, we are not so much different. I wrestle with that same sacrifice.

"I look at my beloved country. You hear about the bloody streets, the barbaric thoughts of men turned loose and brought to fruition on real flesh. But I remember it with that same tainted view as you remember your son. I have my memory of Nuevo Negaldo, the days when children played, when people danced in the streets. When lovers' vows were proclaimed and celebrated. Now I see the gutter flow with the blood of my neighbors. And yet I still love Negaldo. I love Negaldo because I cannot let go of the memory of what I know it was. But someday a sacrifice must be made. Either I kill the memory of my youth and accept the world as it is before me, or we must kill the Nuevo Negaldo that has emerged in order to honor the memory."

The priest sipped on his drink and paused

in his soliloquy. Ed wondered how long Felipe had been preparing this sermon. Was it one he recited every week to any parishioner he came across, or was it written solely for him?

"Or . . . we who wrestle with that will be killed, and the dichotomy . . . will be muted and wiped out from history."

Ed looked across the dusty table at the small Mexican priest. "So, are you always this long-winded when you drink?"

"Yes. Is it so hard for you to imagine a Mexican who can spout grand thoughts and wisdom?" the priest said with a grin as he finished his drink.

"No, I didn't mean anything by it."

"And neither did I."

Silence again.

"Camilla said that you could help me."

"Yes, I can help you."

"Tyler . . . he's alive?"

"Yes, very much so," replied the priest. "Though I do encourage you to think about what I have said. Mexico is not for those with rose-colored glasses. You say that you do not know your son. That may be wise to remember."

"He is my son. I won't leave him down here."

"Good. Very good."

Felipe stood up, adjusted his coat. "Soon, you will come to Iglesia de Señor de la Misericordia. I'll have Camilla tell you when. Maybe tomorrow, maybe a couple of days. Your son is recuperating and needs to get his strength back to travel. I also have to prepare the way for you to get him back to America."

"Why can't I just take him back now?"

"You can't go through the checkpoint with him. That is another thing you will have to let go of here. You cannot trust anyone. Tyler would not make it near the checkpoint alive. No, we'll have to find another way. For now, go back and wait for news from Camilla."

"What am I to do until then?"

"Stay in Hurtado . . . relax . . . I don't know."

"But . . . I am to trust you, just like that."

"Yes, señor, *just like that.*"

"And why should I do that?"

"Because, amigo, I am a priest," Felipe replied with a smile and a wink.

Ed walked out of the cantina after the priest had gotten up and gone to talk with the two men sitting on the opposite wall. He had greeted them like an old friend and quickly sat down, his back to Ed.

28

From across the street, Roberto watched the door of the cantina. He had been near the border crossing when he watched Edward pass through. It was painfully obvious that this was the man he had unwittingly put his hopes on. He looked out of place, unsure of himself, and was doing a paltry job of keeping his anxiety just below the skin.

Roberto followed him at a distance and watched him enter La Terraza. He then leaned against a block wall that provided a little respite from the sun and waited.

From the opposite direction, he saw his uncle approaching. A car came down the street and passed. His uncle went into the cantina and the street was silent.

As Roberto waited, a man approached him and begged him for some money. Roberto pushed him away, and the man stumbled back, caught himself, and walked down the road. A block away the man sat down, lowered his hat over his eyes, and appeared to take a nap.

A half hour passed and the American came out of the bar and started to retrace his steps toward the border crossing. Roberto let him get several yards ahead before he pushed off from the wall and followed.

The beggar who had been dozing stood when he saw Ed coming. He crossed over and went through the motions of asking for money. Roberto saw the gringo shake his head and wave his hand, then quicken his pace. As Ed moved on, Roberto saw the beggar reach into his boot and pull out what looked like a shiv. The scrap of steel glinted in the sunlight. Roberto ran over, grabbed the man, and threw him against the wall. With one hand he punched his shoulder, with the other he covered the man's mouth.

Ed walked on without noticing the commotion behind him.

Roberto pushed the beggar back toward the cantina, kicking at him to speed the man along. Once the threat was stumbling away, Roberto turned and hurried to catch up to the American.

Ed was already halfway down Revolución Street when Roberto got to the corner. He watched from this position until Ed was safely in the US customs office. He then breathed a bit easier and headed for home.

29

Ed made it back to the wall without incident and headed into the pedestrian customs office, a long glass hallway with a swinging gate halfway in. An agent sat at a podium, his energy sapped by the mundaneness of his task, and waved Ed to hurry up so he could return to his daydream. Another agent walked down the hallway, a dog at his side, its tongue hanging out. The man and dog passed him without care.

Ed stepped up to the podium and handed over his passport. The agent opened it up and pressed the photo page over a scanner.

"Are you a US citizen?"

"Yes."

"Anything to declare?"

"No."

The agent's eyebrow narrowed as he looked at the screen in front of him. It was subtle, but Ed noticed the movement. The agent appeared to be thinking about what he saw.

"How long were you in Mexico?"

"Just about an hour or so."

The agent closed the passport and handed it back to Ed, and waved him on.

Perhaps it was nothing.

Ed walked the rest of the hallway and was back on US soil. Nothing had really changed in those fifty steps through the border checkpoint. The land was the same, the air smelled the same. The sounds over across the border were muted by the wall, but he could still hear them. But his anxiety diminished with each step as he made his way back to his motel room.

The customs agent watched as Ed left the office. When he had stepped outside, the agent stood and went to the small office behind the counter. He pulled a cell phone out of his pocket and dialed a number from memory. Someone on the other end picked up.

"It's me. I think I have something," the agent said.

"Go ahead," the voice said.

"A name just came through. Same last name as the kid that dropped that load a few weeks back."

"Was it him?"

"Unless the kid is in his forties, no."

"What was his name?"

"Edward. Edward Kazmierski."

There was silence on the other end.

"Who's on with you?" the voice said.

"John and Amos."

"They inside?"

"No, they're out processing cars."

"Keep this to yourself."

"Already done."

"And Jiménez, we got one coming through at five. Make sure you're working the line then. A blue Pontiac."

"Got it."

The line went dead, and Jiménez returned to his seat at the podium, looking through the glass wall at the auto inspection area, at the endless line of those seeking something in the north. Perhaps his keen awareness would line his pockets a bit, and would help his next trip to El Paso be a little more fun than usual.

30

Every boy is afraid of his father, to some degree or another. A man who says otherwise is a liar. Fear of aggression, fear of disappointment, fear of neglect. Tyler was hiding from the Cartel, had been shot in the back, more than likely sicarios were looking for him, but the thing that was front and center in his thoughts right now was the fear of his old man.

He lay on the cot waiting for some word from the priest. It had seemed like hours since Felipe had left to meet with his father. He thought it was a fool's errand. He was aware that his dad had come down to Hurtado, but to cross the border was another thing altogether.

Eventually, the door to his cell opened and the priest came in, shut the door, and sat down. When Felipe told Tyler that his father had shown up at La Terraza, it was as if his stomach dropped to his feet and the wind vanished from his lungs.

"He's here?" Tyler asked.

"Yes," said Felipe.

"You saw him?"

"Yes."

Tyler's dad had never abused him, unless neglect would fall under that category. After his mom took off to California, they pretty much just coexisted in the same general vicinity of each other. His dad would sit in his chair and zone out into his own world. Perhaps he was missing his wife, perhaps he was just a man who had no idea how to raise a kid on his own and thought that providing the necessities of life was all that was required of him.

In those early years, it was his dad that Tyler missed more than his mom, even though his dad was downstairs in his recliner every night. Eventually, though, the silence became normal, the lack of communication the new reality.

It was no big shock when Tyler had moved out after high school. He crashed with some friends, the ones who seemed cool at eighteen, but then suddenly become burdens at twenty. He drifted down south, chasing after the next free couch to crash on and the next small job that covered an ever-increasing drug habit. When he got locked up in El

Paso, his old man was the only one he had in this world to call, and it was not a surprise that he didn't get any help there.

And yet it was. It *was* a shock to be turned out by his father. The son can commit a thousand sins, but a single sin of the father brings the world crashing down. Tyler didn't blame him for hanging up on him, for refusing to post bail, but he still hated him for it.

Tyler was in jail when he turned twenty-two. It dawned on him that he had been the same age his father was when he was born, and he also realized that if he had his own son, perhaps he would have nothing to say to him in turn. What could he say? What knowledge or wisdom did he possess that was worth sharing? And so the silence would be passed down from generation to generation until there were no more sons searching for wisdom.

"What did he say to you?"

"He asked where you were, if you were alright."

"And you told him?"

"Yes."

"You told him and he just left, went back home?"

"No. He is waiting for the right time to come here."

"I hate to break it to you, padre," Tyler

said, "but my dad is probably long gone by now. You won't see him again."

"And why do you say that?"

"Just because. He wasn't much for getting involved before. I can't imagine that's changed. I'm shocked he came to Hurtado. I definitely can't imagine he wants anything to do with me now."

"I did suggest that to him," Felipe said.

"What?" Tyler said.

"That he should have no illusion of you. That this is reality now. That if he didn't want to help you as you are, he should go home."

Tyler sat up from the cot. His bandaged shoulder burned with each movement as if he could still feel the bullet. "And who am I, padre?"

"Only you can answer that."

Tyler thought about it. He had been down in this hiding place for only a few days, but the pain of the sutures in his shoulder was subsiding and the cold sweats and nausea that he had felt when his body screamed for heroin were diminishing. His sleep had slowly morphed from a coma state to restorative slumber. He sat now staring across the dark, damp room at Felipe. His head was clearing, his thoughts more precise than they had been for years.

"I'm nobody."

"That is not true."

"I'm a junkie who should be dead. Got people who want me dead."

"But you're not. There is at least one person who made sure that you did not end up that way."

"Roberto."

"Yes."

"It's a good thing he knows how to shoot."

"Yes. If you want to get shot without dying, Roberto is the one you want pulling the trigger," said Felipe with a smirk.

"Why do you think he did it? You know, spare me, arrange this with you . . ."

"Roberto believes in an eye for an eye. Or in your case, a save for a save."

"Am I worth saving?"

"All are worth saving."

Tyler stood and ran his hand through his hair. The grime coated his fingers. The movement sent a spike of pain through his body. He winced. "This thing ever going to heal?"

"It will take some time."

"So, my dad, assuming that he isn't halfway back to Kansas already, what's going to happen?"

"I'm working on transportation. Once that is lined up, you'll head out to one of the

139

shelters run by a friend of mine, and from there you'll cross over to America."

"A friend of yours?"

"It's the only thing I can think of. Roberto didn't leave me too many options. You won't be able to cross at the checkpoint here — the Cartel will stop you before you even get close. Juarez is not an option either. They run that too. The chances of you making it to Tijuana without being noticed are next to impossible. If the police stop you, they'll just shoot you on the side of the road."

"So I have to hoof it, is what you are saying."

"It's the best I can come up with."

"So why call my old man?"

"You will be lucky to make it a mile in your condition. You need help. Any coyote will just leave you behind, and any crosser who you are with is just going to do the same thing. Once across, your father would be able to get help from one of the ranchers or police on that side of the wire. The Cartel won't be looking for him. That is the idea."

"Great idea," Tyler said sarcastically.

"No, it's not, but it was the only one we could think of. Or, you can just walk out and try to cross over from here. The border crossing is only twenty blocks away. It would take you about a half hour. But a gringo stumbling to the checkpoint with a bullet wound in his shoulder might not be so . . . inconspicuous."

"I hear you." Tyler put his hand to his wound to remind himself that it wasn't only his pale skin that would mark him. "So, when does this get set in motion?"

"That depends on you." Felipe walked over and inspected the wound, then put his hand to Tyler's forehead.

"I'm ready."

"Tomorrow, we'll see if your father is still around. If he is, I'll bring him over and arrange transportation."

Tyler nodded.

Tomorrow, he'd wait and see if his old man showed up. To see if he was still in Hurtado. He was betting that the answer would be no.

31

Salazar arrived at his house in the southern hills overlooking Nuevo Negaldo. The front gate had a guard shack, and its attendant opened the entry to him, then promptly closed it again. Salazar's car pulled into the gravel circular drive and parked at the front door. Several armed men walked around from shady spot to shady spot. The white cement mansion with red tile roof mimicked the Andalusian architecture that had always fascinated him. He walked across the tile floor into the open air of the solarium where two men were waiting for him. One of his armed servants handed Salazar a cigar, then produced a light for his boss and retreated into the background.

Salazar took time to enjoy a couple puffs of his Cuban cigar and then walked over to his seat. The men in waiting did not speak. They waited until Salazar was ready. They knew the plaza boss liked the theatrics of his position. They were prepared to wait all day, standing like supplicants, but eventually Salazar spoke.

"What did you find?"

"Nada," Arturio said. "We searched the house but found nothing. Nobody but the old man living there."

"And did he tell you anything?"

"No. He said that he hadn't heard from Tyler in years."

Salazar reflected on this and compared it to the news he had received from Lomas. It always soothed his nerves when his lackeys' stories coincided. Trust but verify, an American president once said. It was the only way to run his crew in the plaza.

"Any news on the other side about that third truck showing up?" Salazar asked nobody in particular. None of the men in the room offered a reply.

Salazar thought about it.

Lomas was right, he shouldn't have killed Tyler and Ignacio so quickly. His overreaction at the least sign of betrayal was both his strength and his Achilles' heel. When the two pendejos had slithered back from the border saying the load was lost, he couldn't get them killed fast enough. But then, the load never showed up. It was never reported in the press, by the border agents, by the police. If there was one thing the American authorities loved, it was taking their picture with a seized shipment. They treated it like Christmas.

But that had never happened. Which meant it was still out there somewhere.

And Salazar's boss knew it was still out there.

Everyone had a boss. And as long as the load was missing, Salazar would be on the hook for it.

He sat stonelike in contemplation. He knew his men could never see him shaken by any news they presented to him. Any sign of worry was a sign of weakness. Any sign of fear was an opportunity for an underling to consider advancing their position. A tremor in the voice could topple the fiefdom he had carved out in the Cartel. But he was beginning to be afraid. It started to seep in around the corners.

Sending Arturio and Vicente to Kansas to check out Tyler's old home was a fool's errand, just as it had been to send a crew down to Durango to question Ignacio's family. But Salazar was starting to grasp at straws. No, he shouldn't have killed them before knowing what exactly had happened. Now that he had made his bed, he had no desire to lie in it.

The room held its breath as if it were waiting for a sign to exhale.

A door opened and a suited man walked over to Salazar and handed him a message. Once delivered, the man turned on his heels and closed the heavy door behind him, its echo filling the solarium. Salazar read the note and a smile crept over his face.

"It seems that we have been given a sign," he said.

Arturio and Vicente waited to hear.

"It seems . . . ," Salazar continued, "that a Mr. Kazmierski crossed the border earlier today."

The two thugs looked at each other with puzzled expressions.

"Into Mexico?" Arturio asked.

"No. He was crossing back into the US."

"Tyler?"

Salazar shook his head. "Older man."

"Tyler's father?"

Salazar nodded. "Right here in Nuevo Negaldo. He might be staying in Hurtado. Let's hope he is still there. I want you two to go check it out."

"What do we do if we find him?"

Salazar thought about it. His impulsiveness had gotten him into this bind. His first impulse was to shower the interloper with bullets, but he was aware of his tendencies enough this time to catch that thought. Agent Lomas was assuredly on his way to Hurtado as well, and most likely already there.

"If it's clear, grab him and bring him here. No shooting. Lomas is going to be over there somewhere. I don't need a dead agent right now if things get out of control. Keep it quiet and report back here what you uncover."

Arturio nodded and left on the assignment, Vicente and his giant frame following behind him. Salazar waved over another one of his minions.

"Who carried out the execution on Tyler and Ignacio?"

"Los Diablos, sir."

"Find out who in particular. I want to know who pulled the trigger and where the bodies are within an hour."

"Yes, señor."

Salazar stood and walked around the solarium, billows of smoke trailing behind him. A lifeline had been thrown out to him, but he did not know what it meant. It was something, this gringo from Kansas, that hopefully would buy him some more time to get this mess sorted out.

32

Evening fell, and the western sky coagulated into darkness and the stars shone down on the streets of Hurtado. Ed spent the afternoon in his room, flipping through the few channels on the television chained to the table. Occasionally he would get off the bed to look out the window. The motel was situated off the main road at a slight angle a mile north of the border checkpoint. It was the last building before a stretch of rock and brush ran its way down to the wall, and its orientation allowed Ed to see south from his room. Headlights kept a slow and steady stream coming up the road, an endless line of cars, as if all of northern Mexico was being emptied.

Across the road, Ed could see the restaurant where he had met Camilla. He assumed she was there, behind the counter or waiting tables. Trucks were in the lot, their paint dulled by the desert dust, their undercarriages raised by lift kits suited for the terrain. A border patrol vehicle with a trailer of ATVs was parked along the road, its driver inside grabbing a meal before a long overnight shift.

Hunger eventually overcame Ed, and denying the words of Felipe to stay put, he went outside and crossed to the restaurant.

The air was still and the heat of the day was slowly evaporating into the stratosphere. The gravel grinding under his shoes was the only noise in Hurtado. Ed arrived and went inside, taking a seat at the same table he had occupied the day before.

He fancied that he was becoming a regular.

The border agents were across the room, and several other tables were occupied by random travelers, each going an undisclosed direction, and all content to leave each other in peace. Camilla filled the coffee cups of the agents and then turned, her eyes falling on Ed, and he could see a smile forming in the corners of her mouth. She made her way over to him in a less than obvious way and poured him a cup.

"It is good to see you," she said softly.

"Yeah. Well, you surprised me a bit."

"How is that?"

"A priest?"

She smiled more fully.

"I wasn't expecting that," Ed went on.

"What were you expecting?"

Ed thought about it. To be honest, he was expecting a lot of things when he was walking down to the border crossing earlier that day. He didn't know if he would be robbed, kidnapped, murdered. He was shocked that his entry into Mexico went unnoticed by anyone, and he was more surprised that he had spent time having a drink with a priest.

"I was expecting a person more in line with who Tyler would associate with."

"Mexicans are not all criminals, you know."

Ed took a sip of his coffee. It tasted like road tar.

Camilla put the coffeepot back into the rack near the counter and returned to stand at his table.

"I must admit, you surprised me too," she said. Her words came out with a hint of accent that made even the most mundane words sound like song.

"How's that?"

"I thought that you would be headed home."

Ed stared back at her, waiting for her to continue.

"This isn't a place where most people

stick around."

"So why do you?" Ed asked. The question came out quicker than his mind could catch it.

Camilla thought about the question as if she wanted to give it thorough consideration. "Perhaps the same reason you are staying. My son. I stay here for him."

"He lives here?"

"In Nuevo Negaldo."

"And is there a Mister Ibanez?" Ed braved. He was the father of an adult son, but he wasn't dead yet.

Camilla's smile returned again. "Oh no. No no no," she said. "We are not going to talk about that." She walked back to the kitchen and disappeared. As Ed thought about the brashness of his questioning, she returned with a plate of food that he did not order but was thankful for regardless.

"Eat up," she said and walked away again.

33

El Matacerdos arrived in the coastal town of Guaymas as the lights were just coming on, illuminating an orange sky. He drove straight toward the address that he had been given. It was here he would get instructions for the next job. When he got to the neighborhood, he pulled up to the curb and waited. A face looked out of the window of the small house, disappeared, and then a man ran out the front door. The man came up to the car, a packet in his hand. He was shaking. El Matacerdos rolled down the window and took it from him. The man turned tail and by all accounts was now hiding in a closet, praying that the Cartel had not put his name in the envelope.

El Matacerdos looked at the words on the sheet. He slid it into his pocket, put the car in gear, and drove past the city to the coastal road.

It had been years since he had seen the

ocean, since he had been out this way, so he took the liberty of parking on a bluff overlooking the Pacific and sat on the hood of his car. The water looked dark, the last rays of sunshine reflecting off the waves. He could see people on the beaches below. Kids playing in the sand. Families packing up to head home for the night. They were all living a life so different from his. He sifted through the bag he had bought in town and pulled out the tequila. He opened the bottle and took several very long pulls.

It was a perfect day, but he had work to do.

Two politicians were having dinner at a wealthy patron's home. It had been arranged. The patron's family was currently in a shed somewhere miles from home, perhaps parts of them already dissolving in an acid bath, perhaps watching TV. El Matacerdos would never know. He waited on the street, looking at the property, waiting for ten o'clock.

The house was a sandstone-color adobe with a tile roof and a green front lawn all secured behind a giant black iron gate. Well-manicured trees fronted the entrance. It could have been a hotel. It was nicer than anything El Matacerdos would ever have.

Precisely at ten, as if on cue, the front

door opened and a short pudgy man stepped outside, crossed the lawn, and opened the front gate. He then stood in the open space and waited. El Matacerdos stepped out of his car and crossed over. When the patron saw him, he was visibly sweating, his hairline dripping with fear.

"They are on the back patio."

"*Vámonos,*" El Matacerdos said, more of a grunt than a command.

"My family . . . what about my —"

El Matacerdos pulled out his gun and the man turned and ran down the street.

Crossing the lawn, his shoes sinking into the lush grass, El Matacerdos stepped up to the door and entered the house.

It was an open floor plan and he could see through the entire space to the back sliding doors. Two men were sitting facing the water, cigar smoke slowly drifting up over their heads. One was talking, the other laughing periodically at the story he was listening to. They seemed to be having a good time. Not a care in the world.

El Matacerdos walked across the home, his gun up in case one of them turned around at his approach, but the sound of the water masked any noise he might have made. Within seconds he was stepping onto the patio.

He squeezed off one shot into the temple of the talkative one. The man listening was splattered with blood, his laughs silenced, his mind in bewilderment trying to catch up with what was happening before his eyes. El Matacerdos trained the pistol on him and fired again, a bullet to the forehead.

Waves crashed on the shoreline.

His work was done.

He looked around the patio. It was a good view. More than most could ever expect to have in their lives. He was tempted to sit down and enjoy it but instead made his way back through the house.

Suddenly a side door opened. El Matacerdos turned and trained his weapon on the noise. It was a woman coming out of the bathroom. When she saw the gunman before her, she screamed, her hands coming to her head as she dropped to the floor. Between sobbing and screaming, the woman was begging for her life.

The assassin lowered his weapon and walked out the front door, leaving the crying woman behind with the two corpses. He crossed the street and got into his car. Within the hour he was heading east back toward Chihuahua, where he would await the next job.

34

Ed left the restaurant and headed back over to the motel. The lights of Nuevo Negaldo illuminated the southern end of the road, his back toward the random amber glow of Hurtado's few streetlights. The air was still as he walked into the gravel lot and made for his room at the end of the building. Headlights swung behind him and a white car pulled in slowly, came to his side as its window came down.

Before his brain could process what was happening, a voice came out of the interior. "Mr. Kazmierski?"

"Yes."

"I didn't expect to see you here."

"Who are you?"

"Agent Lomas," the man said, flashing some sort of ID that looked official.

Ed's mind was slow to put the pieces together. He hadn't expected to hear from Lomas again after their conversation on the phone, least of all see him here in the borderlands a hundred miles from any noticeable American population.

"Can we talk?" Lomas said. It wasn't so much a question, but Ed nodded.

The agent pulled ahead and parked the car. He got out and stretched his back as if he had been driving half the day. As he arched his spine, he looked at the beaten-down motel.

"Fancy place."

"There wasn't much to choose from."

"Seems an odd place for a vacation."

Ed shrugged. His gut still told him it was best not to say much.

"So why don't you tell me why you're down here?" Lomas asked as he walked over.

"I don't know. Just thought I'd check it out."

"Tyler?"

"I was curious. Ain't going to lie."

"You said the last time you heard from him, he was in the El Paso jail several years ago?"

"Yes."

"That still the truth?"

"It is."

"Uh-huh."

The men stared at each other in the dark,

light from the last neon tube on the motel sign casting them in a devilish hue.

"Then how did you end up out here? El Paso seems like the place to be if you are looking to fill your curiosity?"

Ed didn't reply.

Lomas walked past Ed toward the road and motioned him over. When Ed got to the road, Lomas pointed south.

"You see that? That's the sewer pipe that Mexico uses to dump its waste. This little checkpoint delivers more drugs in a year than most agencies will seize in a lifetime. They got people thinking about every which way to get their goods through there. Your son was one of them. If you have US citizenship, you can make a nice chunk of cash. Unless you mess up or double-cross the wrong people."

"What's your point?"

"Tyler was a criminal, a druggy, a runner. Mixed up with the worst of the worst both here and over the fence. It's what got him killed. Now, one thing those people don't like more than a runner who loses a load is someone poking around their business. Someone going around, out of place, asking questions about their operation."

"That's not what I am doing."

"You cross over today?" Lomas asked.

Ed thought about the cantina, about Felipe, about his passport being scanned into the customs scanner, about the border agent's subtle hesitation. That was why Lomas was here. He was alerted by the scanner. Ed was easily tracked by a system that was beyond his understanding. There was no use lying about where he had been.

"I did."

"Mind if I ask why?"

Ed took a breath and looked toward the checkpoint.

"Again, just curious. I've never seen the border up close. Just on the news. I was just going to see the wall, come back. But then decided to step over to the other side."

"Last minute?"

Ed nodded.

"Living in the moment?"

"Yeah."

"Uh-huh. And just by the chance of it, had your passport in your pocket?"

Ed didn't respond.

"Mr. Kazmierski . . . do you even know what you're poking at? Do you have any idea the savagery of the people who would not take kindly to finding out you are here? Listen. And listen to me good. You don't belong out here. This is beyond you.

"I get it. He was your son. You might feel

158

an obligation to figure out what happened. But you are starting to mess with a world that you have no experience in. If you know anything, even a hint of a rumor about Tyler, you need to let me know. You need to tell me right now what it is that brought you out here."

"I . . . I guess . . ." Ed was trying to think of words that would extricate himself from Lomas and end this conversation.

"Yes?"

"I guess, I'm here . . ."

"Uh-huh?"

". . . just grasping at straws. Just . . . hoping . . . you know . . . that he's not dead."

Lomas exhaled slowly, frustration evident in his posture. He started walking back to his car. He opened the door and yelled back to Ed. "I highly advise you don't stick around much longer. This really isn't the place to find answers. Leave it to the authorities, we'll find out what happened."

Ed didn't say anything as Lomas pulled out of the motel lot and disappeared north up the road, his taillights drifting into the night.

35

Ed couldn't sleep.

The faded curtain on the motel window flapped in the air conditioner's recycled wake, and yet the room felt as if it were growing smaller in the late hours. He got up and ran some water in the sink, wet his hands and forehead, the back of his neck, and lay back down on the bed.

Lomas had spooked him, and the agent's words heightened his anxiety about the borderlands. Ed really didn't know what he was doing. It was the simple fear of not knowing what was going to happen, and so the mind makes up its own scenario from the bits of stories once heard as well as imagined atrocities.

Why now?

Why after all these years of willfully forcing every thought of his son from his mind was he now here, looking for answers to what happened to him? He had hung up the phone when Tyler called for bail money in El Paso. It didn't prick his conscience then.

It didn't force him to empathize with Tyler on countless previous occasions.

But this time was different.

Why?

It wasn't some sentimentality, as Felipe talked about. He wasn't in Hurtado over some romanticized version of Tyler conjured up from a memory when the boy was young and innocent and new. He wasn't here to save the unsavable. The belief in personal responsibility was as wired into his DNA as his hair color.

Now, lying in the dark at the corner of the world, he felt as if he had a hole in his person that desperately needed repair.

The thought of Tyler being executed. That was what was driving him.

The very idea that he might be an observer of his son's entire existence, from start to finish, from the birthing room to the enigma of a violent end. Man isn't supposed to know both ends of another person's story. If you witnessed the beginning, the end was always to come after your time, or vice versa. To know both, to observe both, was not natural. His drive was to correct the imbalance. To confirm that Tyler was still out there.

Now he knew. Tyler was alive.

Why not go home?

Why was he still here?

Tyler was unredeemable, that was without question.

Or was that just a convenient thought Ed had convinced himself of in order to soothe his conscience to sleep? So many years of dealing with a hoodlum son. He was forever lost. Knowing that he was alive, however, made the shunning possible. Thinking of him dying, and dying horribly, started to break down the wall in his heart that he had erected.

Ed's head swam with the contradictory thoughts. He rose again and walked back to the sink. As he doused his face, lights passed across the room and the sound of a vehicle rolling over the gravel parking lot filled the emptiness of the desert night.

Ed walked over to the window and looked between the crack of the curtains.

An older sedan pulled to the end of the row of motel rooms, turned around, and idled. The lights turned off but no one got out. From this distance Ed could not see the driver through the windshield or if there was more than one person inside. The scrub behind the car glowed red from the taillights, the southern edge of the parking area illuminated like the outer rim of hell.

Ed stood still, the curtain moving slowly, the air blowing on his bare skin, his breathing slow and deliberate.

"People out here don't like outsiders asking questions."

Lomas's warning echoed in his mind as the rear driver's side window came down and a high-beam light shone out at the motel room on the end. The car began to creep forward through the parking lot, its tires slowly grinding gravel as the light wandered over doors and windows. The car stopped two doors down. There was a blue pickup truck parked in front of the room. Ed hadn't seen the owner, in fact hadn't paid much attention to the truck before now. The light went to the truck and fixated on its rear bumper, its license plate, then back up to the motel room door.

The car began to roll forward again, and Ed moved away from the space in the curtains. It arrived at Ed's window, the light beam cutting through the gap in the curtain and hitting the back wall. Ed was frozen in place.

The car moved on.

Ed repositioned himself and watched the car come to his truck, which he had parked next to the motel office. What seemed like a mindless act of walking to his room after getting the key and not pulling his truck in front of his room now appeared to him as a lifesaving action. The car stopped and the light fell on the license plate.

It didn't move on.

The rear driver's side door opened and the man holding the flashlight got out.

He walked up to Ed's vehicle and scanned the interior.

The light turned back down the line of motel rooms.

It was confirmed.

Ed swallowed the fear that was rising in his gut.

They were looking for him.

The shadowy figure walked onto the cement sidewalk and disappeared from Ed's line of sight. He kept his position in the corner, peering out into the night, until almost instantly the figure was at the window. Ed ducked down as the flashlight was pressed against the glass. The light moved around the room, exposing what it could of the interior. The bedspread was still pulled across the mattress. Ed's lack of confidence in the cleanliness of roadside motel sheets proved to be another serendipitous benefit. From all outside appearances, the room looked to be unoccupied.

The man with the flashlight moved on.

He thought of the two men who came into his shop. Were these the same guys?

They would have killed him if Tom hadn't shown up. But there was nobody out here to come and save him if he was found. It was just him.

Ed didn't move, but stayed crouched below the window, holding his breath, afraid each noise would travel and alert whoever was outside to his presence. Soon, however, he heard a car door open and close, and the sound of tires easing onto the road.

He forced himself to rise and looked out, catching a glimpse of the car as it headed south to the border.

36

Ed spent the night seated in the corner, his back against the doorjamb. He drifted between stints of sleep, startled awake by every noise, both real and imagined. Soon the sun rose and the day forced its way between the curtains. He stood and made his way to the bathroom, keeping an eye on the sliver of window, half expecting to see the shadowy figure from the night before peering in.

He quickly shaved and showered and resumed his sentry position near the window.

The parking lot was empty, save for the truck to the room three doors down and his own truck parked by the motel office. He thought he could make out the tire tracks of the desperados' car . . . its marks looking more menacing than all the other marks in the gravel.

The sky was deep blue and cloudless, the

traffic from the south proceeding in a slow trickle as Hurtado came to life.

He checked his watch. It was past ten.

Ed never slept that long, but a full night's sleep is not what he had experienced.

His stomach began to growl and he thought of going over to La Casa de Irma to get some food but decided against it. They could still be out there. Somewhere. The thought of the men in the vehicle the night before waiting for him to step outside checked his desire for food.

He knew they were looking for him. And he knew they found him the same way Lomas had found him.

Hunger eventually won out, and Ed opened the door. The heat from outside blasted his face, and he felt as if he was stepping into hell. Nervously he made his way over to the restaurant. There were a few seats taken, but the place was quiet. He sat at the same table, his table, the same as the night before. The continuity brought him some comfort.

His eyes went to the two customers sitting independently of each other. One was Hispanic, the other white but tanned to a burnt leather by desert life. Neither one was much interested in Ed's arrival, nor appeared to be much interested in anything

167

besides eating their food and being left alone. A man came up and took his order, and Ed was a bit deflated that it wasn't Camilla.

He suddenly wanted to be back in his motel room. He was hungry, no doubt about that, but it dawned on him that what ultimately forced his hand to go outside was the small hope of seeing her in the restaurant. He was drawn to her, not only for the obvious reasons of attraction, but also for the simple fact that she was the only one he had interacted with in Hurtado. Every hour he spent here, isolated with his own thoughts, made even the most benign conversation more valuable.

He placed an order and then told the man that he wanted it to go. When the brown bag arrived, he went outside, crossed the street, and soon was in the safe confines of his motel room.

The TV relayed only two stations, one playing an endless assortment of Spanish-language game shows with wildly obese male hosts accompanied by scantily clad models. The other was running black-and-white shows from an era America had long since left behind. He found himself clicking between the two when his patience with one ran out.

Back and forth.

Hour after hour.

Evening was coming on and with it the growing worry of the men with flashlights returning.

With the last fading lights of day, Ed heard a vehicle pull into the lot. He quickly shut off the TV and ran to his spot against the wall, resuming his surveillance from the gap in the curtain. He heard a car door open and close, though he could not see the vehicle. Soft steps walked toward his door, and then a tentative knocking.

Ed slid to the door and through the peephole he saw Camilla.

His heart both eased and quickened at the same time, as if the organ was bifurcated and supplying different parts of his mind.

He opened the door.

"Hello," he said.

"Hola," she responded, a hint of smile in her dark eyes. "I spoke to Felipe and he says he's ready for you."

"Ready?"

"Yes. He said that I should drive you over tonight. Tomorrow, someone will take you to Iglesia de Señor de la Misericordia."

"Tonight?"

"Yes."

"Is it safe?"

Camilla looked at him as if she was suddenly trying to contain a level of frustration that she was not used to. "I don't know what is going on. Roberto asked me to send you to Felipe, Felipe asked me to bring you to Nuevo Negaldo. Only you three know why." She looked nervously behind her as if the night air was haunted. "Whatever it is you are doing here, I know it is because of Roberto. Roberto is attempting to do a noble thing. I do not know what it is, he won't tell me. All I can do is help him succeed."

"Why?"

"Because, perhaps one noble deed will birth another . . . and another," she said softly. "And eventually, my boy will realize that he can do the right thing by habit."

"Maybe I'm not here for a noble cause?" Ed said.

Camilla's response was quick and sure. "That could be the only reason you're here."

Ed just stood there and nodded slowly. Perhaps she was right.

"But hurry. We must be off."

Ed followed her out, locking the door behind him. He walked to her car and got into the passenger seat. The old car started up reluctantly, the fumes of burning oil filling the interior briefly before clearing out. Camilla put it in gear and headed south.

Behind them, another car pulled onto the road from the far side of the restaurant and began to follow them.

37

They were halfway between the motel and border crossing when the car behind them gained speed and pulled up alongside them. Camilla kept her eyes forward, but Ed looked over at the driver. It was Lomas. The agent waved his hand and pointed to the side of the road, then fell back.

"Pull over," Ed said to Camilla.

She looked at him with stern eyes, but eased off the gas and came to a stop on the shoulder. Lomas parked behind them, got out of his car, and walked up to Ed's door. Ed rolled the window down.

"I thought you were going home," Lomas said, more a statement than a question.

Ed shrugged but said nothing.

"Mind if I ask where you're going?"

"Who's asking?" Camilla piped in, her sonorous voice now edged like a woman who could slice the air with her tone.

Rather than with words, Lomas pulled out

his government ID and flashed it. Ed tried to ease the tension.

"We're just —"

"We're on a date," Camilla said.

Lomas grinned. "Really?"

Ed looked at Camilla. "Really."

"So it's just a coincidence that you're spending the evening with Roberto Ibanez's mother? The same Roberto Ibanez that spent time in jail with your son in El Paso? The same Roberto Ibanez who is a person of interest in Tyler's disappearance?"

"My son had nothing to do with anything," Camilla snapped back.

Lomas ignored her. "What's going on?"

"Nothing," Ed said.

"Get out of the car, Ed."

Lomas stepped back and walked toward his own car. He leaned against the hood and waited for Ed to join him. They stood facing each other. Ed threw a glance back at Camilla. Her eyes watched the pair in the rearview mirror.

"I thought we talked about this last night."

"We did," Ed said.

"I could take you in for interfering with a federal investigation," Lomas said. "I should take you in just to keep you from getting yourself killed."

Ed looked at the agent but didn't respond.

"Because that's how this is going to end if you go off like this. I know you want answers, Ed. I understand that. I've seen a lot of parents drive themselves nuts waiting for word to come back about their kids. Young and old. But you're out of your depth here, and I don't think you realize that. You're going into a war zone. It doesn't run on rules, or at least rules you're used to. For all you know, she's driving you to your execution."

"I doubt that."

"There's your first problem. You can't imagine what could happen."

Ed thought about that and looked at Lomas. His guts were getting tied. The mysterious car from the night before, the shadowy figure in his window flashing the light in the room. But mixed up in all that was the need to keep moving forward, one step at a time. He looked back at Camilla in the car, the border crossing ahead, the ever darkening sky in the south.

"You going to arrest me?"

Lomas pushed off the car, brushed out his pants, and exhaled with a level of resignation.

"You cross that border, I can't protect you. You're on your own."

"Okay."

"Do me a favor? Whatever it is you're looking for, whatever it is you think you might find, you call me when you find it."

"I will."

"These people that Tyler was messed up with, the ones who killed him. They'll kill you in a heartbeat. That is, after they get the answers out of you that you won't tell me. They'll find out why you're pushing."

Ed swallowed. It was as if his throat was closing up on him. He knew if he stood there too much longer, he would succumb to the fear that Lomas was trying to stir up in him. That fear would overpower his irrational desire to see his son, and would drive him a thousand miles from here. Ed stiffened his spine, nodded to Lomas, and returned to his seat in Camilla's car. She didn't say a word as she put the car in drive and headed for the crossing, leaving Lomas to stand and stare at them as they drove into Mexico.

Lomas pulled out his cell phone and considered making a call. He should notify Salazar of what was happening in regard to Tyler's father. If Salazar found out that Kazmierski was in Mexico, and that Lomas knew about it and didn't say anything, there would be hell to pay.

He slowly put the phone back in his pocket.

Salazar's goons would move too fast and too brutally.

The missing load was still out there. Lomas getting a bead on it could greatly improve his position in life.

Twenty-four hours.

Twenty-four hours would give Ed some time to play this out a bit more. He'd probably be back in his motel by morning, and there he could press him for information. Maybe even haul him to El Paso to scare some news out of him.

Lomas returned to his car and sat in the AC.

He'd wait. For now.

The score was worth the risk.

38

They passed through the checkpoint without comment. The amber glow of streetlights reflected off the windshield as Camilla put the border behind them and drove into the heart of Nuevo Negaldo. Loiterers filled the darkened corners of doorframes and sidewalks, flashing neon escaping from the inner recesses of cantinas. The road widened into a concrete boulevard, and emptied into a large plaza with a monument set up in the middle, a dedication to some hero of the oppressed.

Camilla turned west, leaving the statue in the rearview mirror. Ahead, the street closed in again, and from an alleyway blue strobes were bouncing off the cinder-block walls of buildings. Camilla was forced to slow down to a crawl as they passed the police scene.

Ed looked and saw a single police car, officers standing around looking as if they were on break rather than doing any police work.

Farther down the alley, awash in a high-beam spotlight, were bodies scattered on the concrete.

"What the . . ." Ed exhaled.

"Eyes forward," Camilla commanded. Soon they were past the murderous passageway and were zigzagging through tight streets into the bowels of the city.

"Did you see that?" Ed said finally.

"We do not see anything," she said.

"But, back there, in the alley . . ."

"No, and you didn't see anything either."

Camilla took a couple deep breaths and then addressed him as a teacher would address a young pupil.

"You must mind your own business here," she said softly. "Only the bad people end up like that. Only the bad. It's something that you must tell yourself, all the time. Only the bad. Those who break the law, or do things for the Cartel. If they were not bad, they would not end up dead."

Ed looked at Camilla, her face illuminated by the dash lights, giving an angelic glow to her dark skin. "You think that's true?"

"It doesn't matter if it's true or not. It is what you must tell yourself." She breathed in again and exhaled. "Here, you must think that it is safe for good people, otherwise you would go mad. Crazy. There has to be some reason, doesn't there? That is what they tell us. Pay no attention to the dead, for they reaped what they've sown. Look too long at them, and you will go crazy, or the killers will notice you and assume you are a liability. Then, they will come for you, and your neighbors will think that you were guilty too. Only the guilty die here in Nuevo Negaldo. Yes, that is what you must tell yourself."

Ed ventured a question. "And what if that was your son, Roberto, in the alley . . . would you think that?"

"Roberto is no saint."

"I didn't ask that."

Ed thought he saw a drop of moisture form in the corner of Camilla's eye.

"No. I would not think that he was guilty. And I would pray that others wouldn't either."

Ed sank back into his seat and they spoke no more.

The city was unending. The cement store buildings gave way to makeshift housing sculpted on the hillsides from the detritus of generations. Graffiti, trash, and scrap mixed together to create an urban jungle as shallow and haunting as any Potemkin village. Soon Camilla turned onto a wider street and came to a structure that looked like an old hotel. She parked the car and got out, came to Ed's side, and motioned for him to follow. They went inside, past a snoozing desk clerk, and up the stairs.

They walked down the hallway past several doors until she stopped before one in the middle. She took a key out of her bag and opened the door.

"This is where I was told to bring you. There is some food and drink on the table. Stay in the room. This neighborhood is not one that you want to be walking around in." She held out her hand. "Give me your key to your room in Hurtado. Tomorrow, I will gather your things and move your car over behind the restaurant."

The two exchanged keys.

"And that's it?" Ed said.

"That is all I was asked to do."

"Will I see you again?"

Camilla smiled, her shoulders relaxed. "I hope so."

"Me too," Ed said.

"I would have liked to have met under different circumstances," she said.

"Maybe after all this is over."

"Maybe," she said with a coy smile.

She stepped to the door, but before leaving, she pulled a pen and a piece of paper from her purse. She scribbled on it and handed it to him.

"This is the number for the restaurant. There is no use calling me from here, but when you come back, on the other side, you can call for your things. I'll make sure they are brought to you."

Ed took the paper and looked at it. He folded it carefully and put it in his pocket.

"I wish you well," she said as she disappeared down the hallway.

39

Men learn grace from their fathers, which is why there is so little of it left in the world. Mercy? Perhaps a cold mercy, a holding of the fist and a walking away of feet. Seldom the grace of offering an unearned embrace. Of showing a favorable stance to their boys when those boys don't deserve it. Edward had found it too easy to walk away, and considered himself honorable by not entertaining the ruin of Tyler's life for a second longer than he had to.

And now, here he was, in a decrepit room overlooking the squalor of a Mexican border town, pursuing a son he had written off as if he were chasing a ghost. The shacks rolled out to the south, their scrap-metal roofs reflecting the streetlights. The city moved as if by its own will, people and cars and dogs and wind.

Somewhere in this vast sea of misery was Tyler.

His boy. His son.

This was different from Denver and yet the same. Denver hadn't included armed gunmen and lost Cartel loads, covert phone calls and philosopher-priests. But it was familiar, like a vapor in his memory slowly coming into shape. And for the first time in a long time, Ed started to feel that same sense of despair rising up anew when thinking about Tyler, lost down in this murderous city.

Tyler's past deeds, his drug use, his criminal activities, none of that came to Ed's mind as he stared out into the night. Just the feeling of sadness that his own son was lost.

It was foolish, he told himself, trying to rationalize these thoughts.

Tyler was, after all, reaping everything that he had sown. This was the consequence of his own actions.

Ed believed this. He believed this thoroughly.

Yet the thought of abandoning Tyler forever was too much.

Yes, he had turned his back before, but in the corner of his mind, in the subconscious area where all moral truth resides, Ed knew he held the choice to change his mind like a hidden card up a sleeve. He *could* always answer the midnight phone call, could always post another bail, and could always welcome Tyler back if and when he chose to. He always had a choice.

In this scenario, however, his choice was taken from him.

Other people were trying to take his son away from him permanently. Ed wanted the shunning on his own terms, not some barbaric Cartel's. The idea that his son was living and dying at the discretion of another's mercy is what brought up the fear, the horror, the anger, and quite shockingly, the sympathy.

Was he a father anymore? Could he still consider himself such?

Or by ignoring Tyler all these years, had he abdicated that role?

Ed moved from the window and sat down at the small table in the corner that Camilla had filled with food. He unwrapped the tinfoil and ate.

The sounds of the street and the other rooms started filling his ears as his mind slowed down.

Perhaps he couldn't rationalize his actions.

Tomorrow he would see Tyler. He had no idea what he would say to him, or what words Tyler would say back. Or would they just stand there staring quietly at each other? Thinking about that silence scared him as much as any other danger he could imagine.

40

The night air was heavy and thick. The desert heat forced its way through the brick and the cracks, turning Ed's room into a low-grade oven. It was the small hours of the night, the time when criminals start wrapping up their business and honest folk slumber away the last moments before dawn. Ed lay on the bed, arms wrapped around his chest, alternating between a light doze and foggy awareness. He had resigned himself to the fact that he would get no rest in this room, what with the temperature and the things that could be crawling in the corners and shadows. The sweat that leaked out of his body didn't completely dehydrate him and eventually nature came calling. He stood up, walked to his door, and listened. The hostel was quiet.

He opened the door and peered down the hallway. It was dark to his right, save for a few waves of light clawing up the stairwell.

To his left was the communal bathroom, the graffitied door lit by a streetlight shining through a grimy window above the sink. He cautiously walked down the hall as if on broken glass, fought the urge to vomit at the stench and filth of the bathroom, and relieved himself.

He tried to wash his hands in the tin sink, and as he stood there, he looked out the window. It was cracked open slightly and the smell of the alleyway it overlooked wafted into the bathroom. Ed finished up, and as he was about ready to return to his room, a movement on the street below caught his eye. He put his hand to the wall and dared to look down from on high.

If he were Mexican, and more so, a native of Nuevo Negaldo, Ed would have learned the lesson of minding his own business. But he was American through and through, and curiosity compelled him to watch.

A man was half stumbling, half running down the alley. Behind him, from where he had come, two other men rounded the corner in pursuit. At the opposite end of the alley, another shadow moved and blocked the escape route. The man stopped, turned to his two pursuers, and started mumbling in Spanish.

The words poured out of him, his voice a

tone of pleading and supplication. He was bartering, reasoning, begging. Ed could not understand the language, but he could recognize the tone. The pursuers answered with more confident, belligerent bursts of speech. Back and forth they went, the Latin sounds rising up to his window through the heat and the grime and the night. The two men descended on their victim and rained down blows on his body. The man crumpled to the ground, his vocal resonations turning from words to grunts, to sighs, to moans.

The beating continued for an eternity, the men kicking and stomping until there could be nothing left in the man to break. They stopped, pulled the body toward a wall, threw some trash on him, and walked away.

Ed slowly moved back from the window, afraid that even the sound of his breath would alert those below to his presence. When the group of men had made their exit, Ed turned down the hallway and hurried back to his room. Once inside, he locked the door and sat in the chair in the corner, looking out the window at the city below. His sweat had run cold and he was left shaking in the dark.

41

Tyler stood from his cot in the stone room. The radiant warmth of the stones was unabated at night. The cell had the feel of a sauna and he needed some air. The dull ache in his shoulder made sleep impossible, his brain alert and racing with the newfound freedom from chemical influence. He stepped up the stairs to the door, opened it, and peered out into the church. It was empty. Gray moonlight filtered through the windows, shining down into the aisle leading to the altar, illuminating the white-washed stone. He walked across the silent space, his bare feet on the tile, a bead of sweat trickling down his temple.

He was an interloper across a sacred plain.

His left arm felt ten pounds too heavy, as if he were lugging a weighted pack on one shoulder. The gauze and tape pulled at the skin where it had dried with blood.

Tyler moved slowly, struggling, working

out the muscles that had stiffened during his bedridden time. The walls would spin and then settle, then spin again.

He moved to the side where a table of candles stood. There were coins deposited in a tray, burnt ends of sticks, melted wax. He thought of taking some of the money, but the statue of a woman with a raised hand stared down at him from the wall and he thought better of it.

He had seen her image before, tatted on many cholos. Roberto had her image on his right forearm. His gun hand. She would have been looking down on him when Roberto fired the shot in his back.

What a turn of events his life had taken.

With his strong hand, Tyler reached behind him and felt the scar in his back that he had received in the El Paso jail. He remembered that searing pain when the knife went in. He remembered the pain as it healed and eventually became just a mark on his body. The bullet wound in his shoulder felt similar. He knew he would be okay. Felipe had said that Roberto was an excellent shot. Tyler considered lighting a candle for his faux executioner.

Taking the knife for Roberto all those years ago had turned into a lucrative decision. It had made him some money. And now it had come full circle and saved his life.

All he had to do was get to America and all would be good. He'd be set up. That is . . . if the load was still out there. It was big enough to set him up for life. It was too bad about Ignacio, but that was part of the risk. They had both known it.

Three trucks had gone over the border that night. They drove lights out, creeping across the desert single file, Tyler and Ignacio in the rear. The lookouts on the hill radioed to them, directed them through the valleys, letting them know where the border agents were. An hour in, they were on their own, Tyler easing off the accelerator until the two vehicles in front started to drift away, the dust kicked up masking the trail behind them, giving Tyler and Ignacio the cover they needed to turn off when their marker appeared.

They had driven this route before, had planned this for the right time.

Planned for when the load was big enough to risk it all.

Tyler drove west, to one of the isolated rises that jutted from the desert floor, up to an opening in the side of the hill. There was an entrance, an old silver mine abandoned a hundred years ago. Ignacio got out, and

Tyler wedged the vehicle in, the rock walls scraping against the quarter panels, and he brought the truck to a stop inside. He crawled out the driver's window, over the back, to the mouth of the cave.

Ignacio had a cell phone in his hand. He put it on the ground and smashed it. He had called in to the American authorities the route and destination of the other two trucks. The two men headed back to Mexico.

It was a big risk, no question about that, but a score this large could be done no other way. They had to go back. The others in the caravan would be arrested, spending months getting deported; the police would showcase their seizure; Tyler and Ignacio would have escaped being captured.

They would face consequences. A beating more than likely. Questioning. More beating. But in time, they would be back on the trail with their meal ticket stored away in the New Mexico desert for the right time to cash in. They were going to be richer than they ever dreamed of. They just had to be patient, endure the anger of Salazar, wait for the right opportunity.

But what did they know? Ideas cooked up by addicts seem genius to impaired minds.

Salazar allowed no mistakes. There were

too many young men in Mexico waiting for the chance to get in the game, and when Tyler and Ignacio came back to Nuevo Negaldo, Salazar dispatched them quickly. They were dead men. They were dead men as soon as Tyler had turned off trail. They should have just kept driving and never turned back.

Tyler was dead . . . until he had heard Roberto's voice in his ear. *"Listen. I am going to shoot you. You will not die. It will hurt like hell, but fall forward and don't move. It is the best I can do."*

Tyler grabbed a stick from the table, lit it with the candle, and ignited a small votive. He wasn't Catholic, but perhaps the sentiment he had for Roberto would float up anyway. The statue of the lady above the table seemed to mourn in the flickering light.

42

At the hostel, footsteps came down the hall an hour after Edward returned from the bathroom and the observance of the alleyway murder. Someone walked up to the door and turned the handle. It was locked, but a key was inserted on the other side and the door swung open. Two men were in the hall. Ed, still shaken from the grim scene he had witnessed earlier that night, sprang up from the bed and pressed against the far wall.

Two men . . . just like back home. The larger of the two, both in height and weight, hung back watching the entryway. The other came straight in. Despite the darkness, Ed could see the one who entered was wielding a pistol, his white tank top practically glowing in the dark as he moved across the room.

"Miguel, wait out front," the man said, his gun pointed right at Ed's forehead. "You . . . sit down."

The man named Miguel stepped back into the hallway, closing the door behind him. Ed could hear him retreating down the hallway and the flight of stairs. Ed obeyed the order and sat in the corner chair. It creaked when he sat down, sending a bolt through his nervous system.

The man walked over to the window and looked outside, searching for something. He then turned to face Ed.

"You Kazmierski?"

Ed nodded. The man's hand didn't shake. The gun was motionless. Ed stared up at the barrel. He wondered if his eyes would register the flash before the bullet would punch his brains through the back of his skull. Would he even realize anything happened?

"You listen. Tomorrow you will go to Iglesia de Señor de la Misericordia. You will do everything that Felipe tells you. Everything. If you don't, I will kill you and Tyler. You do what he says. You understand?"

Ed nodded again.

"Say it!"

"I understand."

"Good. You will stay inside this room until you are summoned. You understand?"

"Yes."

"You leave this room and I will kill you."

"Yes."

"What?"

"I mean . . . I understand."

"Okay," the man said, returning his eyes to the window and the street below.

As if by some force of will, Ed asked a question.

"Are you Roberto?"

"That's the last time you say my name, gringo," Roberto said, turning to Ed and pressing the gun barrel against his forehead. "You never say it again."

This time Ed acknowledged the order with his eyes.

"You saved him, didn't you?" Ed said.

Roberto stepped back and looked at Ed. With frustration frothing from some hidden wound, Roberto returned to the window and punched the wall with his other hand.

"I committed suicide is what I did," Roberto said.

"Why?"

"Why didn't I kill him?"

Ed waited.

"I don't know. I've been asking myself that question the past couple days."

Roberto moved across the room, opened the door, and looked down the hallway. Content once again that nobody was listening in, he closed the door and returned to his previous surveillance spot.

The gunman's body seemed to slowly relax. The muscles in his neck softening, the tension in the jaw slackening. Ed watched the transformation and could feel his own anxiety start to dematerialize. This was the man who started this whole affair. He would not have brought him down to Mexico just to shoot him in a dirty hostel. The man was wrestling with some inner demon, and Ed waited for him to talk.

Roberto moved close, so close Ed wanted to back up. He lowered his voice as if the room itself were an enemy, waiting to hear his betrayal. Softly, so softly, he said, "I was arrested in El Paso several years ago. They took me into the jail, processed me in. I had done it before, so I wasn't thinking. And when you don't think is when you stop breathing. They sent me into the holding area and I looked around for any of my crew. I saw two of my brothers on the far wall and they saw me. I walked across the room.

"Suddenly, I get knocked over by this white guy. I mean, out of nowhere he slams me from the side and I hit the floor. All I'm thinking at this point is that that gringo is as good as dead. I look up at him but what I see in his face isn't anger, but pure pain.

Behind him was another guy, blood splattered on his face. He had shanked this gringo in the back. But I realized, that knife was meant for me.

"It happened all in . . . like . . . slow motion. Tyler dropped to the floor, blood flowing everywhere, the shiv still sticking out of his back. I get on my feet, and start beating on the other guy until the guards show up and tear me off him.

"They take Tyler out to the hospital or something.

"I mean, he saved my life. I have no idea why. Maybe because he was alone in there and thought he could curry favor with me. Or maybe he thought he'd die and be out of jail that way. I know no one else in there would have taken a knife for me. Not even my crew.

"So I'm left there trying to figure out why he would have done it.

"A couple days later, he's back in the block. He comes in looking like he's half dead. My crew sees him, and I tell them to make sure that Tyler doesn't get messed with. He's not one of us, but we are going to make sure that he doesn't get jumped, you know what I'm saying.

"Goes on like that for a while. He was getting out, so I told him if he needed some work, I could hook him up in Nuevo Negaldo when I got out. Didn't hear from him for about a year. Then he comes looking for me and I hook him up with some runs across the border. Nothing better than having a whitebread American in your pocket. And that was it.

"He's off doing his thing until about a week ago.

"Word goes around that a big load went missing. Salazar is freaking out. He presses down on all of us to find out what happened, but no one knows anything. I bet Salazar was getting squeezed by El Aguila."

"El Aguila?" Ed asked.

"He's the boss. The real boss. Salazar just runs the plaza here in Nuevo Negaldo. This load . . . it must have been something, because they are all freaking out. A couple days later, me and Miguel get a call to do some work. So we drive over and pick up the stooges. Simple job, but then I see it's Tyler . . . and . . ."

"And?"

". . . and I make a stupid choice."

"You saved him."

"I owed him. At least that was what I thought. I owed him. Turns out he's the one who was making the run. He is the reason the load is lost, and Salazar wanted him dead. It's Tyler's luck I was the one picked for the job."

"Luck."

"Curse more than anything. Felipe picked him up after we dumped him outside of Nuevo Negaldo. And now it's your turn to get him out of Mexico. I'm square with Tyler now. I see him again, I'll kill him this time."

Ed sat in the chair and let the whole story process in his mind.

Roberto put the gun in his belt and walked toward the door.

"Remember, gringo. Tomorrow you will go to the church. You will do everything that Felipe tells you. Everything. If I see you again, you're a dead man."

Roberto walked out of the room, shutting the door behind him. Ed was left shaking in the dark stale air of the Mexican hostel.

43

It was around noon the next day when Ed heard a subtle knock on his door. He walked over and pressed his ear to the wood, but could not hear any other sound in the hallway. Cautiously he turned the handle and pulled the door toward him. Peering outside, he looked down the hall, and then toward the floor where he saw a small boy in dirty clothes and an even dirtier face. The child looked up at him with hollow eyes.

"Felipe," the boy said, as if it was the only word he knew.

Ed nodded in understanding, stepped out into the hall, and closed his door. He followed several steps behind the boy as they went down the stairs, through the empty lobby, and out into the street.

The guide turned down the alley and Ed followed. He looked up and saw the window for the bathroom, its glass cocked out on a hinge, its interior hidden from the street by the simple law of geometry. Ed walked on, his eyes moving to the ground and the wall opposite his hostel. He could see piles of garbage and what he was sure was a boot and a leg sticking out from under the bags. The ground seeped with moisture, either from the trash or the body or both.

His nighttime reassurances to himself that the man in the alley was not dead quickly vanished. He stumbled as he tried to process it all. He looked up and the boy was at the end of the alley waving him on. Had the boy seen it? Did he know of the corpse he had just walked by, or had he ambulated around so many in his short life that they no longer were cause for a second look?

"No, and you didn't see anything either."

The boy kept walking, his eyes down but his pace sure and steady. The streets were filling with the noises of the day, and Ed did his best to keep up. After several turns and crossings, the boy ran past a gate and into a church. Ed followed the boy inside.

The cathedral opened up before him and he couldn't keep his eyes from drifting upward into the large expanse. The beauty inside, the result of centuries of devotion, contrasted the living conditions outside in Nuevo Negaldo. Down the middle aisle, Ed could see Felipe walking toward him.

"Welcome."

Ed nodded solemnly.

"Follow me, I will take you to him."

Exchanging one guide for another, Ed followed the priest across the tile, past old ladies coming and going, until they came to a side chapel. Felipe went to one of the walls, grabbed the edge of a giant piece of artwork, and pulled. A door swung open, and the two men went down the steps to the cell. There in the small room, lying on a cot, was Tyler.

"I will give you some time," Felipe said, and he disappeared back up the stairs. Ed wished that he would have stayed. He had no idea how to begin this reunion, and so he did the only thing that he could think of. He said nothing.

The small boy left the church and walked out toward the sidewalk. He placed his hand over his brow and searched the street. He saw a man seated in the shade outside a liquor store and ran over to him. The man looked up at the boy. The boy held out his hand and the man gave him some change.

"I was told to bring a man here."

"Gringo?"

"Yes."

"From where?"

"From the hostel."

"Is he inside?"

"Yes," the boy said.

The man gave the boy another couple coins and shooed him away. The boy ran off in the opposite direction of the church.

"Good."

The man stood, dusted off his pants, adjusted his hat, and pulled out a cell phone. He told the person on the other end that a man from the hostel had been taken to the church. The same hostel Roberto and Miguel had been tracked to the night before. The same church where Roberto's uncle was a priest. The line went dead, and the man disappeared into the streets of the city.

44

Tyler stood.

He had changed since Ed had last seen him. His face had a weathered look, like too much mileage had been put on in too little time. His left shoulder was bandaged, the rest of his torso was bare. The skin was reddened not only by the wound but by many years in the sun. Tattoos slithered their way up his right arm in different designs until they reached his neck. There they sprouted more branches and ran down his chest. Not one large piece done in an exuberant expression but a gathering of ink over many years. Tyler had become a grown man. The memory of his boyish face and body were being overwritten by the person standing across the room. His hair was cropped. His son looked tough.

His eyes were cold.

As cold as the space and the silence between them.

"Dad," Tyler grunted. His posture was entirely unwelcoming.

Ed had tried to prepare himself for this meeting, not knowing if he would feel anger, disgust, disappointment. However, the feeling that came over him was altogether surprising.

He felt sad.

A sadness for the man standing before him.

As if by revelation, Ed realized that without much consideration, he had a part in ushering this person into the world, a world that was more brutal than he had ever realized a week ago. His mind wondered on the thought. He had turned his back on his son, not to fend for himself in a paradise, but to scrap for subsistence in a thunderdome of barbarity. What other outcome could there have been? Where else could Tyler have gone when the doors of his home had been shut to him?

But to harbor guilt would have been disingenuous. At the time, what else could he have done? His son was a parasite slowly leeching the life from him, his resources, all that he had worked for. He had convinced himself that life would be better without his son.

Ed stood motionless just inside the door,

not wanting to move forward but not retreat either. He was paralyzed by not knowing what to do.

Tyler's gaze bore a hole right through him. For an eternity, the two of them lay stranded on the shore of conversation, not knowing how to swim into it.

"Are you alright?" Ed asked. It was the only thing he could think to say.

"For now, I guess," Tyler said.

"Your arm . . . you able to use it?"

Tyler flexed his hand. There was a slight muscle spasm in his jaw. "Yeah, I can still use it."

Ed nodded and looked around the room.

"What are you doing here?" Tyler said.

Ed began to answer but found that he had no words.

"I didn't think I'd ever see you again," Tyler went on. "I figured that was the way you wanted it."

"That's not how I wanted it."

"When I called you from El Paso, that was the impression I got."

"I didn't know what to do, Tyler. I couldn't keep on bailing you out."

Tyler grabbed his shirt from the floor, started to put it on. Ed knew he couldn't begin to imagine what Tyler had experienced since he had left home, but it was obvious that time had been rough on his son. Fights, jail, drugs. It had all mixed together to put an edge on Tyler that made him look and feel dangerous.

"It worked for Mom, just forgetting about us. I figured you decided to do what she did."

"That's not what I was doing."

Tyler moved back to the bed and Ed took a step back. Tyler smiled as he sat down and started putting his shoes on. He seemed to take a little bit of pleasure in unnerving his old man.

"Listen. I'm not looking for some heart-warming moment here. I don't know why they called you. I don't know what they said to you that got you down here. This doesn't really change anything. But here you are, and if you can help me get out of Mexico, fine. But if you want a hug, that ain't going to happen."

"Why did you tell Roberto about Denver?"

"What?" Tyler said.

"Denver. That was what they said on the phone. They said to remember our trip to Denver."

Tyler just stared at him. Something was connecting behind his vacant look. His stone eyes softened for just a moment. "Doesn't matter."

"It does. Why did they mention it?"

"It's nothing. Roberto probably just re-membered a story I told him, used it to convince you that he was legit."

Ed's shoulders slumped. Had he read too much into it? "That's it?"

"That's it," Tyler said, standing and walking toward the door. "Now, Felipe has a way for us to get out of here. Let's find him and get this over with. Then you can go back home. Chalk this up as another mistake."

Tyler walked past him and out into the church. Ed turned and followed, wondering if it was just that.

45

Felipe led Edward and Tyler to the back of the church, through a side chamber where there was a door leading behind the building. He unlocked it and pulled it open, the sunlight flooding the dark space. The opening led out onto a dusty courtyard enclosed by a large stone wall. At the west end, there was a gap in the wall with a drive leading out to the main road. Idling in the cloister was a rusty pickup truck, its tailgate down, its bed filled with all manner of debris. A piece of plywood had been put across the wheel wells, which left a smuggler's pocket hidden below all the junk. The driver of the truck had walked down the alley, his back to the alcove, to have a cigarette. It was obvious that he was deliberately ignoring the goings-on in the courtyard behind him, letting the priest put whatever he wanted into the back of the truck. Camilla's words came back to Ed: *"You must mind your own business here. We do not see anything."*

Tyler walked over to the truck and, with his good arm, managed to slide into one side of the opening. Only the soles of his shoes could be seen as he shimmied around to try to find a comfortable spot. This was going to be a hard ride, Edward thought to himself.

Felipe grabbed two backpacks sitting next to the door of the church. He shoved one between Tyler's exposed feet. He handed the other to Edward. "Good luck, I will say a prayer for you both."

"I'm not sure if I should say thanks about all this."

"You don't have to say anything. Just keep doing. Keep moving."

Ed nodded, shoved his pack onto the truck, and prepared to get in the hideaway. His eyes went back and forth between the truck and the doorway where the priest stood half in shadow. Something was telling him that this ride into the wastelands would be one he wouldn't survive. He wanted to run back into the relative safety of the church. He thought about how he would be sitting at home about this time, in his leather chair with the TV on the local news.

"Go on." Felipe motioned. "You'll hit the migrant shelter in a few hours. My friend is expecting you. You should be in the *norte* by tomorrow."

"Alright," Edward said.

Felipe raised his hand, gave a motion of the cross, smiled slightly, and then closed the door.

Edward climbed into the truck next to Tyler and the suspension squealed as both of them adjusted themselves on the rotting metal of the truck bed. The driver returned from the far end of the alley, pulled a thick canvas tarp over the entire load, and secured it with bungees. Ed could feel the heat of his breath and the claustrophobia set in as the driver raised the tailgate and locked it into place. There was no getting out of this. They were here until the driver let them out, dead or alive.

The driver got into the cab, put the truck in gear, and headed down the alley. The sound of grinding gravel under them soon succumbed to smoother concrete. The truck groaned with each bump as if it wanted to fall apart.

The combination of the sun baking the tarp over him and exhaust fumes from below forced sweat to pour out of him. Edward felt the suffocating air wrap around his body, and he wanted nothing more than to tear out of this junk-pile sarcophagus and suck in fresh air that lay just beyond the walls of the truck. The anxiety built up inside him as his mind raced.

He would die under here. He would die out there.

His head turned to the metal wall of the truck bed and he could see the faintest glimmer of illumination in a hairline crack. Ed managed to reach his hand up and feel the area. He pressed his fingernail into the crack and the material crumbled, a shaft of light hitting his eyes. The small hole had been patched with brittle resin and came apart with little effort. *Thank God for shoddy bodywork,* he thought as he placed his face closer to the opening and did his best to breathe in the outside air.

Edward tried to enlarge the opening over the next several minutes and was mildly successful, it costing him a few drops of blood from beneath his fingernails.

He was able to put one eye close to the peephole and saw the cinder and adobe buildings pass, block after block, crossroad after crossroad. The shadows falling off the buildings gave evidence that they were driving west, and the city of Nuevo Negaldo moved past until empty spaces began to increase more and more as they neared the edge of town. Here on the outskirts, the homes and hovels of block were replaced by abodes of scrap material, wood, aluminum, cloth. The slopes of the western hills populated with a trash-heap existence. In the distance Edward could see large trucks dumping garbage onto giant piles and people milling through the stacks. Like ants on a corpse, they were looking for anything that might add the smallest remnant of value to their scrabbled lives.

The ladder of poverty always has a lower rung if one was willing to look.

The truck drove on, and soon the trash people were behind them and the open desert stretched far to the south beyond imagination. They were out amongst the scrub and dust and rock — whatever might exist out in this scorched earth did so by the most violent of means. They pushed on to the west, on and on, the heat melting his mind as his sense of time escaped him.

"Tyler?"

"Yeah?"

"How far do you think we're going?"

"The farther we go, the better our chances."

It was too hot to keep talking. The only thing Edward wanted was to climb out of the truck and pour cold water on his face. He thought that he would be driven insane.

But then the truck started to brake and turned north off the asphalt highway. The vehicle rattled and moaned as it drove up a country trail, the ruts pounding the truck's suspension and all but breaking Edward's back. The rocky trail smoothed out, and through the peephole, Edward was able to catch a glimpse of a collection of structures clustered together near a dry arroyo. The driver steered them there and parked the truck. He got out, lowered the tailgate, raised the tarp, and walked off to replay the scene of willful negligence that he had enacted back at the church.

Tyler and Edward jimmied out of the compartment and put their feet on solid ground, Edward's balance taking longer than his son's to come back to him. He stepped away from the truck, wanting to be free and clear from the death trap as soon as possible. His hands on his knees, his breath slowly coming back to him.

"This is it," Tyler said. "Come on."

Tyler instinctively went to grab for his backpack and suddenly he snarled in pain. He kicked the bag and stepped off, his right hand rubbing his bandaged shoulder.

"I'll get 'em," Ed said.

Tyler nodded and headed for the camp.

Ed grabbed both packs and followed. By

the time they reached the first blockhouse, the driver had already returned to his truck and pulled out, heading back down the trail to Nuevo Negaldo, most likely glad to be free from the load he carried.

The two gringos walked into the camp, the sun casting the enclosures of the block-houses in oranges and deep shadows. Several men wandered in and out of one of the buildings, food in their hands, their eyes following the newcomers with suspicion. The air was a suffocating mix of offal and a dryness that leeched the moisture out of Edward's sinuses.

It was midday when they had left the church, but now night was coming soon to the valley, the western mountains cutting an hour from the daylight. Tyler motioned for his dad not to lag.

Toward the back of the compound was a large house, and on its front porch stood a portly man with a clean shirt and giant cowboy hat. His face was round and deep-colored behind a well-established and cared-for moustache. He stood erect over the gravel yard and waited for the men to approach. Tyler stopped and Edward came to stand next to him.

And there they stood, Edward and Tyler across from the owner of this migrant shelter, each waiting for the other to make sense of the situation in which they found themselves.

46

The owner looked at the gringos and finally spoke.

"Felipe's men?"

Ed nodded. "Yes, my name is —"

"I don't want to know," the man said with a wave of his hand. "I also don't want my name on your tongue. If you get caught, I do not want you saying it when they rip it out of your mouth. I agreed to give you shelter for Felipe's sake, but that is all."

"Okay," Ed said.

"There are beds inside for you." He pointed to one of the blockhouses. "Five dollars each. You rest up. Tomorrow morning, you will go with the next group. Get you out of here."

"Where is here?"

"About ten miles south of the border. This here is my place. Migrant hotel."

The owner turned and walked away.

Tyler headed off toward the bunkhouse

and Ed followed with all their gear.

The building was brick with dirt floors, and several bunk beds were jammed inside with barely enough room to maneuver. Several of the beds were occupied with haggard men who stared at the gringos as they walked in. The room fell silent, apprehension thick like fog. The owner suddenly appeared in the doorway.

"Over there, against the wall," he said. "You take those two."

Ed nodded and stepped over. Tyler took the low bunk, propped his feet up and stretched out as if it was just another day in the life of a world traveler. Ed looked toward the opposite side of the building. All eyes were on him. His nervousness kept building. Not a word was said by his new roommates. They just studied him from the shadows.

"They think you are criminals," the owner said. "Why else would two Americans be here?"

"I guess there is no use telling them we're not," Ed said.

"Speak for yourself," Tyler grunted.

"I don't care. If you are or not, you will both be gone tomorrow."

Edward kept his gaze on the vagabonds across the silent space.

"Are we safe in here?" Ed asked.

"Of course you are," the owner said.

"You sure?"

"Yes. You see, these men here, they are not criminals," he said in a sly tone. The owner stepped out, leaving Ed, Tyler, and the migrants to blink at each other over the chasm of foreign thoughts and customs and fears.

47

Felipe walked up the aisle of the church, his footsteps sliding across the tile filling the vaulted space. The church was practically empty except for the errand boy who was putting things away in a side chapel and an old woman lighting a candle at the votive table. Evening was coming on and the duties of the past several days had worn on him. He was tired, and so he sat down in one of the pews in front of the altar. Tomorrow would bring about another chance to do a good thing, whatever or whoever might bring it his way.

The boy who retrieved Ed from the hostel walked over to where Felipe was sitting and asked if there was anything else the priest was in need of.

"No, I believe that is all for today," Felipe said.

Before the words were out of his mouth, Felipe heard the trucks pull up in front of the church. Most of the parishioners arrived on foot, so the noise was noticeable as well as out of the ordinary. The roar of the engines reverberated in the catacomb of the cathedral. He couldn't tell how many there were, nor how many people were in each vehicle. The sound of slamming doors told him there were many of them. All come to serve justice to the traitorous priest.

It was destined to end like this, was it not?

The boy's face transformed, a mix of fear and guilt in his stare as he looked toward the entryway. The large mesquite door swung open and two long shadows were cast down the aisle, the headlights of the trucks flooding toward the altar and illuminating the young boy's eyes. Footsteps, a closing door, more footsteps. Felipe thumbed each bead of his rosary in cadence with the advancing men. The sounds stopped just behind him, and Felipe turned slightly and saw a tall man kneel, cross himself, and then sit down in the pew behind him. A larger man stood in the aisle gazing at him.

Arturio and Vicente.

He had known these boys when they were younger. Now their younger selves were gone, executed by the killers they had become.

"Forgive me, Father, but you have

sinned," Arturio said.

Felipe said nothing. He said nothing, but looked up at the boy. The boy looked back.

"You can go home. And remember, whatever happens, you are forgiven."

The boy wilted under the words, the change in his pocket turning to lead, his guilt not only transforming his eyes, but also weighing down his slumping shoulders. The boy ran down the aisle and out of the church. Felipe closed his eyes in prayer.

"Perhaps while you are at it," Arturio said, "you can ask your God how he felt about Judas."

"The boy is not a Judas."

"I wasn't talking about the boy, padre. It is you. The traitor. The friend who betrayed with a kiss. For that is what you have done, is it not? Betrayed us? It is, isn't it?"

"I'm afraid you are mistaken."

"You are right to be afraid. Now, I can't imagine that the word in Nuevo Negaldo did not reach your ears all this time. That one of Salazar's shipments was dropped."

"I pay no attention to the dealings of Salazar," Felipe said.

"I doubt that is true. You have heard this, yes? Of course. It was your nephew who was assigned to . . . eh . . . ," the tall man crossed himself again, ". . . disposal duties. The men who tried to steal from Salazar. But it seems that a very odd occurrence has happened."

"And what is that?"

"It seems," Arturio said, "a father has come to Nuevo Negaldo. And for some reason, he came here. To your church."

"Many people come here."

"Not too many gringos, I bet."

"I have helped many of those in need in my time here. It is my duty to do so," Felipe said. His shaking hands continued counting the beads.

"Is it your duty to betray Salazar?"

"My duty . . ." Felipe breathed deeply. "My duty is to help those in need."

"I am in need, can you help me?"

Felipe turned in his seat and faced Arturio, "If you truly seek help from God, then yes, even you."

"No, padre. I do not believe that God can help either of us today," Arturio said as he sat back in the pew, arms spread out as if reclining someplace less holy, scraping the crud off his boots with the kneeler. "Now, I am only going to ask you once. Answer quickly, and Vicente will be merciful. *Comprende?*"

Felipe turned back toward the altar and bowed his head again in prayer. He focused on the martyrs, thinking upon them for strength to endure what he knew was inevitable. He prayed to keep his silence, to be strong in his own martyrdom . . . but his ears were tuned to Arturio. He nodded.

"The Americano . . . why was he here?"

Felipe exhaled. The church was breathless.

"Where is he now?"

Felipe shook his head.

"Vicente!" said the tall man, snapping his fingers.

Vicente moved quickly for his size. He seized Felipe by the shoulders of his frock, dragging him from the pew as the priest tried to get his feet under him. Before Felipe could stand, Vicente drove his fist into his stomach. An explosion of pain tore through the priest's innards, and he dropped to the floor. He gasped for breath and saw blood spittle on the tile as he clawed for air. Vicente followed up with a swift kick that flipped Felipe over on his back.

"What was he doing here?" Arturio yelled. His voice echoed off the stone walls.

"Please . . . ," Felipe gasped, ". . . all I ask . . . is not here. Do not do this here."

Arturio held up his hand to halt Vicente from another strike. "Where is he now? Is he here?"

"No."

"Then where did he go?"

Felipe said nothing.

"Take him outside."

Vicente bent down, grabbed Felipe by the collar, and proceeded to drag him down the aisle. With one hand gripping the priest, he pushed open the door with the other. There were more men outside waiting by the trucks. Vicente went outside and the doors closed behind him.

Arturio leaned back in the bench and put his feet up on the pew in front of him. From the corner of his eye he saw the old woman cowering next to the votive table. Her face was to the floor, her hands over her ears. Her body may have been present, but her eyes and ears would prove no witness. He grinned sadistically at her, put his feet on the floor, stood up, and walked over to her. He picked up a lighting taper, lit the end, and then tossed it on the floor before her.

"*Chiquita!* Light another candle for Felipe, yes?" He laughed at her as he turned and walked outside to join in on the activities.

48

Salazar sat in his chair, the cigar smoke creating a gray cloud that wafted in the dark room. He looked out the window of his study over the city of Nuevo Negaldo. It was his city. His plaza. He had earned it. And now it was all unraveling. He could feel it. The tension in his shoulders was creeping in from a fear hundreds of miles away.

It was all but time until the boss came knocking, and every minute the pressure increased until Salazar was at a point of boiling over. When his phone rang, his stomach turned. He knew who it was before he spoke.

"Yes."

"Why has this not been fixed," El Aguila said.

"I have it under control," Salazar said.

"From what I hear, you are losing control. I gave you Nuevo Negaldo because you led

me to believe these things wouldn't happen."

Salazar thought about the words. Even
though he told himself this was his plaza, it
never really had been. He had just been the
warden. He had climbed only so far.

"Where is the load?"

"We will find it."

"You told me that already."

"I need more time."

Over the receiver, Salazar could hear El
Aguila clipping the end of a cigar, the sound
of a powerful butane lighter igniting it, and
the deep inhalation of the man on the other
end.

Salazar had mimicked the same action in
his own little fiefdom. His little plaza. He
felt hollowed out, like he was just playing
boss.

"The Americans did not seize all of it, Salazar. If they did, not only would I already
know, but so would half the world. They
would have paraded it on the news like a
trophy. Where is that extra truck? No small-
time pendejos have it. They would not be
able to move that load without me knowing
about it. That leaves only two options, Salazar. Either the load is sitting out there
somewhere, or perhaps . . ."

Another deliberately long toke on the cigar

from the boss.

". . . perhaps you are sitting on it yourself."

"I am doing no such thing," Salazar shot back furiously, then checked his tone. This was El Aguila. One always had to respect him if they wanted to stay in good standing. "I would never steal from you."

"No?"

"I am grateful for all you have entrusted me with. I would never do that."

"Yes, yes, I have heard these words from others many times before. But sooner or later, there is always the temptation —"

"Never from me."

"Maybe. But then again, I can't have loads go missing through my plaza. It makes me look weak. It makes me look vulnerable. Do you think I am weak, Salazar?"

"No, señor."

"Do you think I am vulnerable?"

"No, señor."

"Do you think I am forgiving of incompetence?"

Salazar said nothing. He suddenly found it hard to breathe. It had been a long time, but he felt his hand begin to shake as he pressed the phone to his ear. A bead of sweat ran down his temple.

"Who were the couriers, Salazar?"

He told him. He told the boss why he had

chosen Tyler and Ignacio. Tyler, for his American citizenship, his appearance. Ignacio because of his loyalty. He told the boss how the two had made countless runs before without incident. He told him how the path was cleared well in advance, which border agents were patrolling the sector, which rancher he had paid off to get the trucks through. The location of the drop point. He told the boss everything.

"And you trusted them?"

"Yes."

"They told you they would never steal from you?"

"Yes . . ." Salazar whispered, his own words coming back to him, now ringing foolish.

"Find that load, Salazar. Find it soon. If you do not, I will need to find someone else to run my plaza."

The phone went dead.

Salazar put his phone away. The cigar in his hand had burnt down, but in his anxiety he had crushed it between his fingers.

He stared out at his city and saw it slowly slipping from his grasp.

49

The waves of campfire light filtered through the single-pane glass of the window above Edward's head. He could not sleep, and after watching the glow move hypnotically in the dark, and tiring of the slow snoring of the other men in the bunkhouse, he stood and walked outside.

The owner sat in a lawn chair out in the yard, his dark face illuminated at times by the fire, then disappearing again. Next to him was a cooler, in his hand a cerveza. A radio sat in the dirt and from it played a melody of accordion and horn music that to American ears was synonymous with the mysterious country to the south. The owner eyed Edward as he made his way to the fire, and when Ed arrived, the owner stood and produced another chair, which he placed across the pit from his own. Ed sat and his eyes went from the stars overhead to the dancing flames and back again. Eventually the silence was so overwhelming that the owner reached into the cooler, pulled out a cold bottle, and tossed it to Ed.

"Thanks," Ed said.

"De nada."

Ed popped the cap and took a small sip.

"Those men inside, you know them?" Ed said.

The owner sat silent and calculated his words. "No. I don't know them. But they are like so many others who have passed through. And there will be more tomorrow."

"You see a lot?"

"Always."

The fire crackled and embers rose into the sky, ascending like small imitations of the stars above them.

"Thanks for letting us stay."

"Like I said, Felipe asked, so I said yes."

Ed nodded and took another sip.

The owner seemed to be wrestling with himself. He appeared as a man with a burning question but who also knew full well that his curiosity would do nothing more than give him an answer that he did not want to have. The silence between the two men felt like an iron weight that wanted to be cast off.

"That other one," the owner finally said, "he your boy?"

"Yes."

The owner nodded.

"What about you, any kids?"

"Yes. I have a son."

The two drank from their respective bottles.

"He live here with you?"

The owner shook his head. "He's in the north, with his mother."

"You see them much?"

"Not as often as I'd like, but yes. Your son, he is the reason you are out here. I know that. What other reason could there be," the owner said, more to himself than to Ed. "What other reason would you have not just gone through Juarez, or Nogales, or Nuevo Negaldo."

Ed eyed the owner as the Mexican continued with his mental conversation.

"You need to get him across without eyes seeing him. That makes him dangerous. That makes you both dangerous. These other men will leave tomorrow and they will be gone. Or if they are caught and deported, they will come back again to make another crossing. But you two, your presence will linger here, and that is dangerous to all of us."

"We can go now, if that is what you want."

The owner came back out of his trance

233

and looked at Ed. His eyes reflected the fire, but there was no malice in them, just the look of a man who had seen much.

"No. You are here. Better that you had not come, but there is no changing that."

The owner stood, grabbed another piece of dried wood, and placed it on the fire. In another time they could have been two cowboys on the frontier, relaxing after a long day's ride.

"I can see why Felipe helped you. There is a brotherhood amongst fathers, though his children are not his own. I can see that. I can understand what you are doing. It's why I help these men that come here. They go north for the same reason. Same reason as you. Some of their sons are there. Some of them are back south. They attempt the crossing to sacrifice for them. I did it for my boy. There is no life here. Not anymore. Only death and the masters of death. Life cannot grow here, and so these men go searching to find life and pass it to their sons in some form."

"Up until a week ago, his life was none of my business," Ed said.

"Until a few hours ago, your life was none of mine," the owner said.

"How hard is the crossing?"

"It's difficult, but not impossible."

"He's hurt. Ty . . . my boy. His shoulder."

"It's why you're here, I guess. He needs to keep up or they'll leave him behind."

Ed nodded and put his beer down on the ground. "I guess I better get some sleep then. I'll be lugging his pack for him."

"Good night, *americano.*"

Ed left the owner by the fire where his silhouette glowed demon-like in the high desert.

50

It was impossible to know what hour it was in the morning when the call went through the bunkhouse for all to rise and get outside. A flatbed pulled into the camp with the sound of a machine about to embark on its last operation. The migrants filed out into the dark, securing a spot on the vehicle, some sitting cross-legged, others stretching out. Ed followed his son out into the blackness, climbed aboard, and sat amongst the others. The truck jerked into gear and set off into the wastelands.

They watched as the bunkhouse slowly faded from view, swallowed by the never-ending horizon which could have stretched untouched to the ends of the earth. The owner sat where Ed saw him last, next to the campfire, his feet on the cooler and his hat pulled low over his eyes. He would sit there in Ed's memory until the end of time.

The ruts and rocks of the road jostled the

men about, but they swayed in cadence with the rolling country. Only Ed struggled to balance himself with each lurch of the truck. He had never learned the skill of riding bareback on a steel machine. The men were driven under the stars, far away from any man-made lights. Out where man had given up the idea of setting down roots.

Time passed and the moon moved toward the western mountain range.

The truck drove on.

Ed looked at the faces of his fellow passengers half painted in the moonlight. Most looked out into the wilds, lost in thought. One man lay dozing against the cab, his cowboy hat held in his hands, finding sleep as easy as a baby in a rocking cradle. Ed locked eyes with another man who just sat there with a half grin on his weathered face.

Ed didn't remember the man from the bunkhouse. He must have come on the truck. He was caught in the other's trance when his son nudged his shoulder.

"He asked me why we're here," Tyler said.

"What did you tell him?"

"Not much."

"Who is he?"

"Julio," Tyler said, and with the sound of his name spoken, the man nodded his head and kept the same sadistic grin on his face.

"He's the coyote."

"The what?"

"Coyote. The guide. He's taking us across the border."

Julio slowly turned his head from Edward and spit out into the passing country.

"Once we get across the wire, we'll lose them," Tyler said. "I don't trust him here on this truck, I'm sure not going to trust him out on the trail."

"What do you think they'll do?"

"The others are fine. They're nobodies. Farmers. Laborers. It's him I don't like. Pretty sure he can figure out why we're here. Probably thinks there's money to be had by us. Bounty, reward, something."

"You think there is?" Ed asked.

"Not for him. If he manages to get us turned over to Salazar, he'll be shot just like us. They won't owe him anything. Doubt he thinks that, but it's what they'll do."

Ed nodded slightly and kept his eyes on the road behind him.

The truck turned abruptly, almost throwing several of the men off the back. It burned a path across the hardpan and then came to a stop. Julio stood and started to shout in Spanish, pushing several of the men to get up, on their feet, vámonos. They all dismounted and gathered in the brush, waiting for the man to lead them to the promised land. Ed gathered both of their packs and followed Tyler at the back of the group. The truck turned in the dust and disappeared, a similar scene as the one that had brought them to the migrant shelter.

They walked for a short time, crested a ridge, and headed toward a mesquite thicket on the downward slope.

Julio shouted out more commands and the men spread out, taking up plots of ground under the limbs, each to their own thoughts. Julio took the highest perch, sitting by himself, the others sprawled out, waiting for the sun to crest the eastern hills.

"What are we doing?"

"We are waiting for daylight to cross those hills there. On the other side, we'll hole up until evening, then make the crossing at dark."

Ed looked at Tyler for more explanation.

"They can't just drop these guys off at the wire. Mexico and the US are both pushing out space on both sides of the line. We're about ten miles south of the crossing. It's better to walk those miles when you can at least see where you're stepping. Then, once it's dark, you're all set to go."

Ed nodded, the realization that this was so planned out coming as a shock to him, even more so that Tyler knew the system as well as he seemed to.

"Happens every day. In fact, I'd bet there's several groups within a couple miles of us," Tyler went on.

"Each one led by a guy like Julio?" Ed said, motioning slightly toward the coyote, who continued to stare at him from his perch.

"Yeah. There's no shortage of them."

Ed tried to relax on the hard ground. His body was already hurting, and the idea that this was just the beginning slowly started to make itself known in his mind.

51

It was morning twilight when they heard commotion on the ridge above them. An older man and a young boy walked down from the hilltop carrying with them several jugs of water. The old man had a cowboy hat on his head, long black hair, and beads around his neck. His white button-up shirt was pressed and seemed to glow in the dark, making his descent easy to track. His boots planted firmly into the hillside with each step. The boy accompanying him walked meekly behind him like a small dog, handing out water containers to the disheveled group. Words were exchanged in Spanish between them. The old man walked over and squatted next to the nearest migrant, exchanged a bit of conversation, and then proceeded to perform a blessing over him. Once done, he stood, shook the migrant's hand, and went on to the next one.

"He's a priest," Tyler said.

"Yeah, I figured that," Ed said.

To Ed, it was starting to seem that Mexico was filled with only bandits and holy men. Perhaps they were one and the same.

The priest stood and walked up to Julio. The coyote was still commanding the high ground above his flock of border crossers. As the old man started the ritual, Julio shook his head and waved the holy man away. Instead of a blessing, the priest held out a jug of water, which Julio took without complaint.

The holy man made his way down the slope and stood before the two gringos. His face was puzzled and in his deep-set eyes it was apparent that he was both confused and a bit amused. He spoke rapidly in Spanish, but his intonation made it clear that he was asking a question of Ed. Ed nodded, and the man slowly launched into his rehearsed uttering, moving his hands over the space above their heads, blessing the two on their journey *al norte.*

The priest finished and walked down the hill, disappearing into the brush. The young boy, now empty-handed, sat on the ground and rested his feet, waiting for the priest to return. The migrants stood and followed the priest, all except for Julio, who remained seated, watching the procession from his perch. Ed and Tyler followed the others.

About a hundred yards down the trail where the hill ended in a dry arroyo, they found the priest standing in front of a makeshift shrine, the others standing behind him, their heads bowed in prayer.

"Toribio Romo," Tyler whispered to his father, "the saint of border crossers."

Ed looked at his son.

"Supposedly, if you get lost in the desert, Romo appears to rescue you and helps you find a job in the US."

"They think this helps?" Ed asked.

"They'll take any help they can get. There are shrines all over. Toribio ain't so bad. The ones who pray to Santa Muerta are the ones who give me the creeps."

Ed looked at his son again as a question.

"Death."

They both looked on as each of the migrants produced small trinkets from their packs.

"This land is haunted by saints," Tyler said. "The narcos pray to Malverde, these guys to Toribio. But the nasty ones worship Muerta. Our lady of death. Violence is a religion, and she is their holy mother."

"Do you get into all this?" Edward asked.

"It comes and goes. When Roberto shot me, I prayed to whoever out there might be

243

listening."

The migrants lined up and began laying down small offerings on the shrine. When they stood, the priest handed them a little card. On it was a picture of Toribio. A sanctified baseball card. The old man handed one to Ed, who looked at it and put it in his pocket.

The priest led the procession back up the hill to the makeshift camp. Dawn had arrived and the holy man and the young boy disappeared above the ridge to wherever it was that they had come from.

Ed watched them leave and then turned to see Julio staring at him, the same old sadistic grin on his face. It made him uneasy. The man had less the countenance of a coyote and more that of a vulture. Julio got up, put his bag on his back, and led the way down the arroyo, past the shrine, and north to the distant hills.

They all followed quietly, each to their own thoughts.

52

Roberto had laid low at his mother's house for several days and he was as restless as ever. By now, Tyler should be on his way to America. He was now in the past. In a couple days it would be behind them. Everything would be back to normal and his stupid act of keeping a gringo alive would be lost to history.

He didn't sleep that well, his body tossing and turning, his thoughts racing through every possible fallacy in his plan. How he could be exposed. How he could be found out. Perhaps this was his new life, wondering at every moment if Salazar and the Cartel had discovered that he'd double-crossed them. The drive out to the airstrip almost pushed him over the edge, his anxiety making him sick. He was becoming paranoid. If he was stoned, he could blame the drugs, but he was stone-cold sober, and the only thing driving his hysteria was the fear of a bullet smashing his skull when he least expected it.

It was just after dawn when his cell phone buzzed on the table next to his bed.

"Yeah," Roberto said.

"Roberto, outside. You need to come quick," Miguel said.

"What is it?"

"Outside. I'll tell you when you come out."

Was Miguel going to be the one to end it? Would he take more than two steps out the door before his friend blew him away? At least he had the courtesy to do the deed outside his mother's house. Roberto grabbed his gun and tucked it in his pants.

He peeked through the front window. The street was empty save for the old Buick and Miguel wedged behind the steering wheel. He stepped outside and felt the first rays of day hit his face and nothing else. Miguel waved him over, to hurry up and get in.

"What is it?"

"It's your uncle."

"What happened."

"It's bad, bro. They did him bad."

The two headed for Iglesia de Señor de la Misericordia, Miguel aggressive on the corners as he weaved through town. He had received a call on his cell from one of Los Diablos. They drove through the crowded streets until they reached the church. A large group of people who had begun their day heading to work had traded that idea to form a crowd in front of the gates of the church.

Miguel pulled the car over and Roberto was out and running before they came to a full stop. Miguel stayed behind as his partner broke through the mob of gawkers. Roberto knew what he would find when he saw the crowd, but he was not prepared for the excess that Salazar's men had gone to.

There, on the gate to the churchyard, hung Felipe, in cruciform pose. His throat had been slit, and his tongue had been removed. His body bore signs of other mutilation, a testament to those who would dare cross the Cartel in the future. From Felipe's right hand dangled a rosary, wet with blood, the silver cross spinning slowly. On the ground below his left hand was a crucifix. Pinned to his chest was a sign . . . TRAIDOR.

Roberto fell to his knees.

He couldn't breathe. All the air was sucked out of his lungs and he gasped for oxygen. He had seen carnage before, but never against his own flesh and blood. His uncle Felipe was not murdered, he had been butchered. Had been used not as a priestly example, but as a Cartel signpost.

Rage filled Roberto's body. His anguished sob turned to a bellowing scream as he stood, pulled his pistol from his waistband, and waved it at the crowd.

"¡Vámonos!" he screamed at them, pointing at one face after another. "Vámonos!" he yelled as a tear came down his cheek.

The small crowd dispersed in every direction, racing away like rats.

Roberto turned back to his uncle. He stepped up, untied the ropes holding him up, and took him down from the gate. Blood slopped on his hands and shirt. Miguel now came to help.

"What is going on, Roberto? Who would do this?"

"Salazar."

"But why?"

Roberto looked at Miguel. Now with the blood of his uncle on his hands, he hesitated to bring another person into the knowledge of what he had done. His fear and paranoia over the past several days was well-founded. They knew that Tyler was here. They knew that Felipe had harbored him. For all he knew, Salazar's men had grabbed Tyler and dragged him off. He couldn't bring Miguel in on it.

"It is best if you go, amigo. They are after

me now."

"You?"

"Yes."

"Why?"

"I can't tell you."

Miguel shifted on his big feet.

"Whatever happens, Roberto, you my boy."

"I can't let you do that."

"You have no choice."

"All right then."

Roberto and Miguel picked up Felipe and carried him into the church. They laid him in the aisle before the altar. It had been a long time since Roberto had stepped foot in his uncle's church. The altar of El Señor de la Misericordia loomed large over them. Roberto crossed himself, the once natural act now feeling foreign to his muscles. He bent down and kissed his uncle's cold forehead. From his pocket he pulled out the coin with the Holy Mother on it. He placed it in Felipe's hand.

Help Me to Alleviate All the Suffering
and Misfortunes in the World

"I will avenge you, *mi tío.*"

Roberto took Felipe's rosary and put it around his own neck.

He stood, walked out of the church with Miguel behind him. Sirens could be heard coming from somewhere in the heart of Nuevo Negaldo, late as usual. The two got in the car and Miguel pulled away from the church.

"Where to, amigo?" Miguel asked.

Where to exactly? If Salazar already had his hands on Tyler, then it was game over. But if Tyler and his old man had left the church, then they would be on the next leg of their escape. He knew where that was. There were dozens of launching points for running people across the border, but he was confident he knew which one his uncle would have sent Tyler to. And if that was the case, then the men who killed Felipe, the men who Roberto would make pay for what they did, would be on their way there also.

Roberto told Miguel where to go, and Miguel hit the gas.

53

They walked through the morning, single file through the scrub and rock, dust kicking up at each step. They made their way into a patch of mesquite where the shade provided a place to rest. Trash littered the ground all around them, the remnants of countless travelers who had gone before them — old clothes, empty bottles, wrappers from energy bars long since consumed. They lay down and made beds of the earth as best they could.

Snoring from the Guatemalans drifted through the branches, coughing from the Salvadorian. Julio had disappeared into the thicket, and for all Ed and Tyler knew, the coyote was staring at them from a hidden vantage point.

"If you need to sleep, go ahead, I'll keep an eye out," Tyler said.

"That's all right."

"No, I mean it. We are going to be laid up

here for a little while. It's best to get the rest as you can get it. You're carrying two packs. And besides, you look like you could use it."

"I was young once," Ed said, almost apologetically.

"Just get some rest."

Ed adjusted his back on the hard earth, his backpack under his head. He was so fatigued that he cared little for what might be crawling around in the undergrowth. His body was not ready for this march. The others in their party looked like they were built for labor, but his softness around the middle and his lack of regular exercise were soon apparent not only to him but to the others as well.

Tyler, even recovering from the bullet wound in his shoulder, still benefited from being young. The tap of unearned energy had been shut off for Ed many years ago. Before he knew it, he was asleep.

Tyler took off his shoes and socks and checked his feet for blisters. They were holding up all right, but more than likely they wouldn't be by the time they hit I-8. Then again, he didn't have to worry about working in the fields soon after. He would find a nice quiet spot to hide out, rest his body, and make his plans on what to do next. He looked over at his father asleep next to him.

The scenario before him was one that he never in a million years would have imagined. For most of his adult life, his father had been a stranger. After leaving home, he never saw him. Never interacted with him. Never thought about him unless he was in a jam and had no one else to call. He had made that call several times when he needed cash for bail or for a fix. But the last time he called, when he was jailed in El Paso, his old man had hung up on him.

Tyler was sure at that time the two of them would never speak again. Life would roll on to its end, neither being the wiser to the fate of the other.

After El Paso, then to Nuevo Negaldo, he'd wandered through life.

He sometimes wondered about his mother, if she was still alive in LA. When she left, he had missed her, but now she was more or less a mental curiosity. His dad, however, he found he thought about less. Maybe it was because, during all those years together after his mom had left, they had learned to live together without noticing each other.

But now, here he was. His father. Trekking through the borderlands back into America via a path for unwanted people and castaways. Tyler knew that that was what he was, or what he was to his father. A castaway. Unwanted.

So why was his dad here now?

He looked at him lying on the ground. He looked old.

Yesterday, when he was standing in the cell of the church and saw his dad walk in, he wasn't sure what to think. He had created a hatred for his old man over the years, a hatred seated on the idea that he had been abandoned. Had been set adrift in the world without any support.

But to his surprise, deep down in his gut, he also was filled with a sense of comfort. A feeling of home. A feeling that even as a grown man, his father was there, and where his father was, safety was too.

It wasn't a sentimental fairy-tale feeling that washed over him, but a deep-rooted assurance, a calmness. A memory that as a boy, where his father was, he was protected. Perhaps that was a feeling that never died and existed to old age. Whatever it was, Tyler was glad his old man was here with him.

He had convinced himself that he did not need his father. But now, together in the borderlands, he wouldn't wish him away to save his life.

Tyler took a swig of water from his dwindling supply and gazed north past the group of men. They were all pushing north for the dream of better things. Better lives. In the north, there had been no life for Tyler. He had burned all bridges, scorched all the past that he had had by means of crime and drugs and resentment. But his future was not in Mexico. He could not go back there. He would not survive a week.

He was a man stuck between two worlds, two different worlds that he neither belonged to nor could hope to survive in.

No, there was no future back in Mexico. The only way forward was to go back home.

And the only way he could do that, he knew, was with his father behind him, watching his back. It was the only reason to keep moving forward. He had nothing else. He had no one else. And for this moment he would take what he could.

His dad might turn his back on him again. Might shut down into himself. Might kick him out and shun him once this was all over, but for now, he was with him, by his side, and he would use that feeling for however long it would last.

"I don't trust him," Ed said.

They were sitting across from each other

resting their tired legs, the tree above them that took root a century before providing a bit of shade. The wood was petrified gray and stood like bones stuck up amongst the rocks. The sky overhead was cloudless and the white sun was climbing low on the horizon.

"Julio?" Tyler said. He sipped a small amount of water, enough to cut the dryness of his chapping lips.

Ed nodded.

"Best not to," Tyler said. "These coyotes would bury their own mother under a rock if it meant they would gain by it."

"Have you seen him before?"

"No."

"Never? I mean . . . with all the people you were running?"

Tyler looked at his father with serious eyes. The look was accusing but also filled with a sense of astonishment at Ed's lack of understanding.

"I never ran people."

Ed just stared.

"There are hundreds of people like Julio in Mexico. And hundreds more to take his place if he ever dies out here. He leads these poor people north not out of some mission but simply for cash. He doesn't care about them. He'd turn tail and run south at the first sign of trouble. Probably done it before. It really is the wolf leading the sheep."

"I just don't like the way he keeps eyeing us," Ed said.

"Probably thinks we are worth more than what he is getting paid."

"What do you mean?" Ed asked.

Tyler looked toward the group of migrants seated about ten yards up the wash from them. Julio sat perched high on the berm, his usual vulture-like gaze looking down at them all.

"He's probably making a couple hundred a head to get these guys up to I-8. They'll jump in a car and head off to wherever they are designated — Chicago, New York, LA. Julio will then cross back over, get paid, and wait for the next run. It's decent money down here. But guys like that are always looking for a better score."

"That a problem?"

"Depends on how much Felipe paid for our transport. The coyotes see white skin, they figure they can pinch some money on the side if they feel like they're getting shorted on the deal. Russians, Ukrainians. They sometimes come through here. Can't imagine he's seen many Americans though."

"Do we have anything to worry about with him?" Ed asked.

"Not as long as he thinks we ain't scared of him."

"And you're not?"

"No," Tyler said.

Ed thought about the situation. If he was honest with himself, he would admit that he was scared. The wilderness surrounding them was filled with a deadly assortment of nature's creations that could kill by bite or sting. Up on the ridge sat a man who looked ready to cut their throats. But what made Tyler so calm? He appeared to be at ease in the company of these men, as if this was a walk without peril.

"Can I ask you something?" Ed said.

Tyler nodded.

"You ever . . . have you ever . . ."

"What?"

"Killed someone?"

Tyler looked at his father, then turned and looked at Julio, then back again. He brought the water bottle up to his lips and took a slow deliberate drink. He capped the bottle and placed it back in his bag, stood up, and offered his good hand. Ed took it and got to his feet.

"Don't worry about him," Tyler said. "He's not going to try anything. And if he does, I'll take care of it."

Tyler stepped off and headed back to

camp. Ed thought about what his son might mean. *"I'll take care of it."* To what extent was his son capable of protecting him? It made him nervous to think that he and Tyler were vulnerable, but it made him just as nervous to think that they weren't. That Tyler was willing and able to violently take care of himself. Ed slung their packs on his already aching back and started for the trail.

By noon they reached the base of the mountain they had been pushing for and made their ascent. The rocks slid with each step and Edward's quads and calves started to burn and stiffen until he thought he couldn't go on anymore. Soon they came into a clearing with a sharp overhang and Julio instructed everyone to stop. They would camp here until dark. To the north, the range spilled on.

"There's America," Tyler said as he sat down.

It was impossible to tell where one country stopped and another began. Fatigue won out over curiosity, and the snores returned to the group.

Their bodies slept beneath the shadow of stones, their minds kept walking in their dreams, one step in front of the other, an endless trek north through the boot heel of New Mexico toward a magical road that would carry them to their future reward.

Ed had never felt so old. His body ached, and even though he was beyond exhaustion, he found he could not sleep longer than a few minutes at a stretch. The others snored on and he realized he was from a different world than theirs, one that a walk such as this would not make the same. These men bored through the world like diamond. Their strength was hewn into their bones from birth. They did not complain, or if they did, they kept the words inside. On the trail they were quiet. In their sleep, they rested with contentment on their faces as if they were back home in their own beds.

But the earth did not comfort Ed. The rocks seemed to shift under his body, poking him in his back, his legs, and he struggled to get comfortable but found no relief.

Tyler sat with his head down. His vigilance to keep an eye on Julio had disappeared along with his ability to keep his eyes open. The coyote was asleep higher in the rocks, his feet stretched out into view above them like half a corpse sticking out of stone.

Across the plain, rock formations and mountains sprouted up like islands in a sea of prairie scrub. How many groups of men were huddled up in the crevices waiting for night to fall to make the journey *al norte*?

In his mind's eye, Ed envisioned hundreds of men sleeping in the wild, a smorgasbord of meat for any wandering carnivore that would go against its nature and venture out into the heat.

Sleep came.

Sleep left him.

Ed stared into the cloudless sky.

Here, the day passed without recognition as it had for many years of his life. Ed never imagined this place existed, but it would go on existing until the end of time. Tomorrow, another person would lie where he was now, gathering their strength for the coming night's journey. And the day after. An endless train of wanderers desperate for a life with more abundance than from whence they came.

His life had been easy, he thought. What struggle had he actually had?

He looked at Tyler. His son in this place as a consequence of his own choices, yes, but also helped along by Ed's shunning. And here they both were, on the side of a prehistoric rock formation, hiding from the rays of the sun, walking north like refugees.

54

Roberto and Miguel drove into the staging area of the migrant farm. There was a vehicle parked in front of the bunkhouse and several men were offloading their packs and milling around in the shadow of the building. The endless stream of travelers, the next batch collecting and readying themselves for their turn to cross the wire. Roberto drove his car behind the bunkhouse and parked. He sat there until he saw the owner walk out of his house and stare at them. Roberto got out of the car and waved him over.

"Roberto, it's been awhile," the owner said nervously. He always had a subtle crack in his voice when one of Los Diablos or Cartel members came out to his place. "What can I do for you?"

"It's about Felipe."

The owner steeled his eyes and waited for what Roberto had to say.

"Did he send you somebody?"

"Yes."

"Are they still here?"

"No, they left last night."

"Who was the coyote?"

"Julio," the owner said.

Roberto's gut tightened. Julio was scum. Loyal to no one, not even Salazar. Miguel had gotten out of the car and walked around the bunkhouse. Something had captured his attention.

"Has anyone else been out here since they left?"

"Anyone like you?"

Roberto nodded.

"No."

Roberto looked at Miguel. His partner was staring at the dirt road winding through the desert. He turned to see what held Miguel's stare. Two black vehicles were approaching. These weren't traffickers or locals. They didn't use nice cars to transport the human fodder that were being driven north. These were Cartel vehicles.

"Anyone call you, asking about Felipe."

The owner now was becoming more uneasy.

"No. Nothing. Roberto, what is this about?" the owner said. As soon as the words came out of his mouth, he too saw the trucks pulling into his property and his nerves came undone. "What did you do? What did Felipe have me do?"

Miguel hurried back to the car, opened the trunk, and pulled out two guns. He hollered at Roberto and tossed one to him. The owner started backtracking to his house, stumbling over his feet, and crashed through the front door as the trucks skidded to a stop, a dust cloud falling over the bunkhouse, the migrants inside staring out at the scene unfolding before them.

The doors of the first truck opened and Roberto saw Vicente step out. He knew these were the men who killed his uncle. He knew it like a dog knows when food is out for the taking. Vicente spotted Roberto eyeing him from behind the bunkhouse, raised a weapon, and started firing.

The gunfight that erupted echoed among the hills, shattering the silence of the desert. Roberto and Miguel on one side of the cinder-block structure, Arturio, Vicente, and several other Cartel men using their trucks as shields on the other. The bunkhouse was riddled with bullets, while screams of the migrants who threw themselves on the floor were drowned out by gunfire. They were caught without hope in the cross fire.

The shooting intensified, both parties firing blindly from behind their secure positions, relying on luck rather than aim to hit their targets. The first lull in the firefight came on as weapons were reloaded, and several of the migrants sprinted out of the bunkhouse in search of a better hiding place. The Cartel thugs, either frustrated at not getting clear shots on Roberto and Miguel, or out of simple bloodlust coursing through their veins, opened up on the fleeing men and mowed them down, gunshots ripping through their bodies that fell like rag dolls into the dirt.

From the house, a blast from the front door echoed through the clearing and one of Arturio's men was violently thrown against the side of the truck. He fell to the ground dead. The owner pumped another round into his shotgun and fired again.

The Cartel, suddenly exposed on their flank, ran for cover and were left open to Roberto and Miguel, who both stepped out and fired relentlessly.

Lead flew in every direction, undiscerning in its target, slicing into flesh and steel and dirt. The owner continued to fire, taking out Vicente's kneecap, while a shot from Roberto finished him off in the throat. When the rifle went empty, Roberto pulled his pistol from his waist and started to shoot. His expertise with the handgun proved lethal to everyone in his sights. Each shot found its mark.

Doc Holliday reborn.

The Cartel members all fell, most not turning from the owner's shots in time to react to the deadly accuracy of Roberto until it was too late.

And then all was quiet.

Roberto still stood as the dust and burnt gunpowder began to drift away on the breeze. His heart beat violently in his chest, the blood forcing the veins in his neck to swell, the adrenaline threatening to ooze out of his pores. He looked around.

To his right, next to the bunkhouse, lay Miguel. His face and shirt were red with blood. Roberto couldn't tell where he was shot, or how many times, but he knew that it didn't matter.

His friend was dead.

Roberto reloaded his pistol and walked toward the trucks, now nothing more than scrap metal riddled with bullet holes. He stepped from man to man, checking for life in each one. They were all dead. But one person was missing. Arturio.

Where was he?

Roberto slowly walked around the last vehicle and saw the man sitting in the dirt, a gun in his right hand, attached to an arm that had been shot apart and lay limp on the ground. Arturio was struggling for breath. Roberto stepped in front of him, raised his gun, and stared at the man. He thought of the image of his uncle crucified on the gates of Iglesia de Señor de la Misericordia. He wanted Arturio to suffer, he wanted to prolong the man's death, to gain vengeance for Felipe, and now Miguel. But it was not to be.

Arturio breathed his last and slumped to the dirt. Dead.

Roberto looked to the main house. Through the open front door he could see the owner lying on the floor, his boots sticking straight out onto the porch. He had no desire to investigate how many bullets the man had taken.

He walked behind the bunkhouse to the Buick. He wanted to load Miguel's body up and take it back to Nuevo Negaldo, but his friend was too big to move. He would have to leave him here for now. Respect for the body would come later.

He got in the car and pulled out of the camp. Behind him, a few faces of the surviving migrants peered out in terror from the bullet-ridden bunkhouse.

55

Roberto reached the asphalt that stretched across the Mexican landscape, its route running parallel with the border some ten miles north. He came to a stop, the sun beating down on the hood, his eyes staring blankly out the windshield, the sweat from his forehead beading up and running down his temple. His heartbeat slowly coming back to normal after the gunfight.

Miguel was dead. There was nothing to be done about that now. He would tell the other Los Diablos how he had fought; his brothers would honor Miguel's memory. But for now, the magnitude of his situation came crashing over him. He had killed Salazar's men. They would eventually find him and kill him. There was no reprieve from such action.

Why was this so complicated?

Miguel's death left a hole somewhere inside him. Could he have killed Miguel if it had ever come down to it? If Miguel had stood in his way to riches and power, would he have not simply removed him too?

No.

A voice inside him said no as soon as his mind asked the question.

Miguel was family. A twisted family born in the streets and by the shedding of blood, but family nonetheless. He and Miguel had stood side by side against the shower of bullets from the Cartel. Only family would do that. Family was stronger than money and power. He would have taken a bullet for Miguel, just as Miguel had taken bullets for him. And Tyler, having taken the knife for him in El Paso, had become family. That's why he did what he did. It was for honor. For family.

The Americans thought there was no pride in the Mexican mind, but they were wrong. Dead wrong. Thinking on these things, Roberto gripped the wheel until the pressure pained his fingers and he pried them up, then punched the dashboard in fury; once, twice, again and again until his knuckles started to swell. He screamed, a barbaric yawp that carried out of the open window and echoed across the desert plain.

But what to do now?

He could go west, cross the border in Nogales, hide out in the US. He was a dead man in Nuevo Negaldo. Salazar would order him to be killed on sight. No matter what his brothers might do to defend him, and he knew they would die defending him, it would be just a matter of time before he would be caught unawares. Slipping into America he could make his way to Phoenix, Albuquerque, maybe even LA.

But what about his mother?

The sun was just overhead, the day halfway through. She would leave work tonight, drive back home, walk into her house. Would Salazar have men there, waiting inside, waiting for him to arrive? Would they seek revenge on her, using her body as a substitute? The thought snapped him back to reality.

Roberto put the car in gear, turned east on the road, and drove like a madman toward Nuevo Negaldo. He wouldn't leave his mother to walk into a trap. He wouldn't run to save himself and leave her to suffer in his place.

If he was going to his death, he would make them earn it.

56

Roberto drove to his mother's home, went to his room, and pulled a milk crate from under the bed. He retrieved several boxes of ammunition, some clips, and some cash. Stuffing them into a bag, he went to the kitchen, took a pull of tequila, and ran his head under the sink. The dirt, gunpowder, and sweat from the migrant shelter poured from his skin into the sink.

He had called his mother on the way, telling her to go to her cousin's in Deming for a few days. She said that she would and he hoped that she would keep her word. He could hear the worry in her voice as if she was trying to leap through the phone and comfort him through the airwaves.

"No, Mama. Do not come home. It is not safe. I will let you know when you can come home."

Perhaps it was a lie. The only way she would be able to come home was if he was dead, and the Cartel had proof of his body. Until then, she was in danger. They would use her to get to him, or use her for the simple fact of satiating their sadistic sensibilities. She would be safer in the north.

The shot of liquor hit his head and calmed his nerves as he stared down at the dirty water circling the drain.

Losing Miguel was hard. He would trade Miguel for Tyler any day. Riding back to Nuevo Negaldo without his overweight body sleeping in the passenger seat had been like trying to walk after a stroke. Nothing felt right and half your body was numb as if it were missing. Now he was on his own, nobody to watch his back.

His mother's home felt like both the safest place and the most vulnerable at the same time. Roberto had no idea if Arturio or Vicente had called in Roberto's location at the migrant shelter, or if Arturio had notified anyone else of the firefight before he died. It didn't really matter. He was a dead man walking.

Just like Tyler.

Stupid choices had doomed everyone. Felipe, Miguel, his mother, himself.

If he would have kept his head on a swivel when he had walked into the El Paso jail all those years ago, he would never have come across that gringo. Never have felt obligated. Never have been duty bound to foster the cancerous relationship that years later would send his life into this downward spiral.

Life on the streets in Nuevo Negaldo was never easy, and many of his crew had died quickly and suddenly, usually from making poor choices — stealing from Salazar, snitching to the *policía.* They had it coming. They knew the moment that they had signed their death warrants. But to think that his fate was sealed when Tyler took that knife in the back was a kick to the gut. It was out of his control, and in Mexico, if you didn't have control, you lived and died by the whim of another.

Roberto had fought and bled for control. He knew the rules of the neighborhood, the plaza. He picked up the bottle of booze and threw it against the wall, its glass shattering into a million pieces. He turned off the water, grabbed his bag, and went out the front door, his head swimming with thoughts of cause and effect, the linear progression of fate, of unwanted circumstances, of duty-bound codes of honor, of the thoughts that philosophers pondered for thousands of years.

He was just as distracted as he stepped

outside the front door as he had been when he had walked into the El Paso jail. So distracted that he didn't notice the truck turn onto his street without braking, its passenger window down, a gun pointed at him. He only came to when the first shot echoed through the neighborhood.

57

"Hey . . . you . . ."

The voice was heavily accented and the words came out cautiously. Edward opened his eyes and looked over at the two men seated next to the rock wall. They had their bags cushioning their backs and the look on their faces said they simply wanted to talk.

"You," one of them said, *"norteameri-cano?"*

Ed stared back at them. The two said several words in Spanish between each other and smiled large, toothy grins.

"Sí," Tyler said, then spoke to his father. "They wanted to know if we're American."

"Where are they from?" Ed asked.

"Qué?" the man asked.

Tyler sat down next to Ed and spoke to the men in Spanish. The conversation went back and forth and Ed was surprised at this hidden skill his son had.

"They're from Guatemala," Tyler eventually said. "He's Juan. The other one is Luis."

Luis spoke to Tyler with a flurry of words and Tyler answered back. The two started laughing hysterically.

"What's he saying?"

"Wants to know what we are doing here."

"And what did you tell him?"

"I told him I brought you out here looking for a wife."

Edward grunted and Juan started spitting words again.

"He wants to know if we're related."

"He's my son . . . ," Ed said, looking at the two men. "Son." He repeated the word slowly as if the speed would aid understanding.

"They know," Tyler said.

Luis pulled an old wallet out of his back pocket and took a photograph out. He looked at it reverently and then passed it over to Edward, speaking rapidly.

"That's his boy," Tyler translated. "He is back in Coban with his mother."

Edward studied the picture and then handed it back with a nod. Luis kept the conversation going and Tyler translated it to his father in English.

"They crossed over into Mexico a couple weeks ago. Then, took the train north. The beast —"

"Beast?" Ed asked.

"It's what they call the freight trains that run north. They pile up on the cars and ride them as far as they can."

Tyler prompted Luis and he continued.

"There were three of them when they started out from Coban, but one of them didn't make it. He fell asleep on top of the train car and rolled off." Ed watched as the two men made the sign of the cross at the mention of the incident. "They assume he's dead. He was Juan's brother. This is the third time they have made this trip.

"They were going to cross near Laredo or Juarez but thought they'd have a better chance away from those places. They have heard the stories. All the murders."

"Where are they headed?" Ed asked.

"Atlanta. Construction gigs."

"What's his son's name?"

"His son?"

"In the photograph, what's his son's name?"

Luis responded with a sentimental tone. "Carlos."

"It must be hard, leaving him . . . ," Edward said before he realized what he uttered. Tyler translated the words that more than likely stung his own mouth. Why would his own father be concerned about another man leaving his son behind?

"Yes," Tyler translated. "But he is a growing boy, and eats too much. So he goes to work. What father would he be if he didn't support his son. It's from him that his boy will learn about family, responsibility. He goes as an example to him."

The conversation ended when Tyler stood up and walked away, leaving Edward and the two Guatemalans unable to do anything but stare at each other. Ed watched his son walk down the path that had brought them up the mountain. He got to his feet and followed him. Twenty yards from the makeshift camp, Tyler was leaning against a rock looking out over where they had come.

Ed walked up and again struggled with knowing how to start a conversation. "Why did you tell Roberto about Denver?"

Tyler looked back at him, his eyes set hard, but didn't say anything.

"Why that? It just . . ."

"What?"

"I'm just wondering why you would talk about that."

Tyler folded his arms and grimaced when the movement caused a pain to shoot in his shoulder. He looked to be considering his words carefully.

"In jail, you have a lot of time to talk. Not

much else to do. After I got out of the hospital, Roberto made sure I wasn't messed with in there. We got to talking, 'bout this and that. He asked me if I ran with anyone. I said no. He then asked if no one ever had my back."

Tyler spit on the ground, then continued.

"It just came out. I said one time, I got real scared. Long time ago, when I was a kid. Mom had taken off. So we went to Denver. At the end of the day, I thought you took off too. I thought that was it. I remember that feeling. Feeling . . . hopeless. I had no idea what was going to happen. For that brief moment, I thought I was forever alone. Then . . ."

"Then what?" Ed asked.

"Then you were there. You hadn't left. You didn't take off. I felt like at that moment, that one moment, you had my back. That we were going to be okay."

Ed didn't say anything.

"I miss that, you know? I miss having that feeling."

Tyler stood up, and walked past his dad back up to the camp, leaving Ed with a hole in his gut for all the years that had passed between them.

58

Mercy is a dangerous proposition.

By staying the hand of justice, it's more than likely you'll get repeated acts of violence by the guilty. Mercy means trusting your enemy won't return in the middle of the night to bash your skull in. Mercy gives power away. It's a daily act of suicide against your best interest — all in the hope that the world would be made anew.

The only thing more dangerous than mercy on this particular day was Roberto Ibanez with his pistol, and he was doing everything but bestowing mercy.

If he had been a cowboy in the Old West, a marshal, a lawman, his legend would have been born on this day. In El Paso, way back, the infamous "four dead in five seconds gunfight" had turned Marshall Dallas Stoudemire into folklore. Wyatt Earp at the O.K. Corral. Heraclio Bernal, the Thunderbolt of Sinaloa. Roberto Ibanez would have joined their ranks by nightfall.

But he was just a poor Mexican gangbanger on a backstreet in a border town facing down armed gunmen of the Cartel. The world would not remember him.

The first shot buzzed his ear and ricocheted off the front of his mother's house. Instantly he had his pistol out and fired at the passing truck, his bullet finding its mark on the gunman. He ran for cover to the stone wall bordering the yard as the truck zoomed past, hit the brakes, and came to rest sideways fifty feet away. The driver and rear doors opened and three men jumped out, each with automatic rifles. They began firing on Roberto's location. The stone wall was turning to dust with each impact, a huge cloud forming in the street as the men kept up the assault until their magazines were empty.

At the lull, Roberto ran across the street, his arm outstretched, firing as he went. He clipped one of his attackers in the neck, the man falling back against the vehicle as he desperately clawed at his throat, the blood leaking beneath his balaclava. His next shot hit the second gunman in the shoulder, spinning him around and down onto the pavement. Roberto missed the final man by fractions as he took cover against the wall of the neighbor's shack.

The lone attacker had reloaded and waited for a sign. Roberto did the same. Two men catching their breath, waiting to see what the other would do. Across the street, Roberto could see his bag lying on the ground in front of his house. He had only the bullets that were left in his clip.

He was lucky that most of Salazar's lackeys didn't know how to shoot. Their lessons had come from movies and television. They shot up targets while half drunk on tequila and were more focused on imagery and bravado than discipline and accuracy. Roberto knew it didn't take a hail of gunfire to kill a man, just one meticulously placed shot.

He turned and ran between the shacks to the next street over, then started running west. He worked to get behind the last gunman. He ran, past one house, past another. Through the gap between houses, the hitman fired his weapon when Roberto raced past. Roberto kept moving, then heard the truck start up and the sound of squealing tires. The assassin was going to drive him down.

He turned left, through another dusty yard, hopped a fence, and was now two blocks away from home. He crouched behind a Dumpster and waited. Soon, he saw the truck pull onto the street. Driving slow, the barrel of the rifle out the window, the man was checking between the gaps in the buildings.

Roberto slowed his breath from the run. Worked to calm his beating heart.

The truck came even with the Dumpster.

Roberto stood, squeezed off a shot, and then fell back down.

The truck sped up and then coasted down the street, veering off the gravel, and hit a pole. The engine kept running, but there was no movement from inside the SUV. After waiting several moments, Roberto moved up to the vehicle, gun raised, and looked through the driver's window.

Dead.

One shot through the temple.

He opened the door and pulled the body of the driver out, then walked around and removed the passenger, who had been the first to expire. He got in, backed away from the light pole, and drove back to his house. The two bodies were still on the street. One was dead, the other man was dragging himself off the road. Roberto ignored him and pulled up in front of his mother's house. He gathered up his bag and headed out.

In just a couple hours he had taken out a plethora of Salazar's goons. He had no idea how many more the day would bring his way, but he was going to be ready for each and every one of them. He had to find a place to hole up, get some cover, and think about what to do next. He could never go back to his mother's house. Not as long as Salazar ran the plaza.

59

His cell phone rang, and El Matacerdos pulled it from his pocket and held it to his ear.

"Are you finished?" the voice said.

"Yes."

"Any problems?"

"No," he said. He brought the bottle up to his lips and put it down again. He knew that the voice on the other end was going to send him off on another hit before he was done self-medicating.

"I need you in Nuevo Negaldo."

El Matacerdos began to plot the route in his head. It was almost a full day's ride. There was nothing more that he wanted but to lie on the bed, drink himself into a stupor, and sleep off the events of the past several days. No matter how many jobs he executed, it always took several nights to lose the vivid image of the kill from his memory. He had learned that the best post-execution routine was to hole up in a motel, pass out drunk, and wake up more debilitated from a hangover than the thoughts of another person murdered.

But now he would not be able to go through the ritual.

The boss was sending him north, to the border town.

His boss questioned the long silence. "Is there a problem?"

"No, I will go."

"I will message you tomorrow morning."

The phone went dead before El Matacerdos could reply.

He gathered his things and looked around the room, making sure that all was as it should be. He would never set foot in this spot again. That was the way of the sicario. Or of the sicarios who wanted to live to old age. He took the bottle of tequila to the sink and dumped it. If he couldn't put it in his gut today, no one would.

He walked out of the room and got into his car, pulled out onto the road, and started the trek north.

There was a stop to make first.

It had been too long since he had made a visit, and even though it was against his better judgment to stop, he felt like he had to. Normally he would set up a clandestine rendezvous, but he didn't have time. He had to get to Nuevo Negaldo as soon as possible, but going to the border town always filled his mind with a sense of fatalism. Murder and death were everywhere and it took people without prejudice. He didn't know if he would be back. So he decided to risk it.

About an hour northeast of Hermosillo, into the Sierra Madre, El Matacerdos pulled his car off the highway and onto a gravel road that led up to a small town. He drove slowly by the old abandoned buildings and crumbling adobes that littered the hill. The road became tighter as he ascended, the houses encroaching more and more on each side to the point that the rearview mirrors threatened to scrape the block walls. As he crested the rise, the rocky drive widened out and he parked the car. At the end of the road was a small dwelling that looked to have been pieced together from the ill-fitting bones of other houses. Through the windshield he watched and waited.

The sun beat down on the top of the hill, and El Matacerdos was ready to turn back, when the front door opened and a small boy ran outside. He was being chased by a small dog yapping at his heels. The boy's yelling echoed amongst the old buildings as he played with the mongrel in the street.

El Matacerdos took the pistol from his shoulder holster and put it in the glove box. Then he opened the door, stepped out of the car, and slowly walked toward the boy. The assassin's body cast a long shadow on the ground until it was hovering over the youth. The dog sat and stared but didn't bark. The boy looked up.

"Papa!" he squealed as he stood and wrapped his arms around the sicario's waist.

"How are you, Pepe?"

"Good. Where have you been?"

"I've told you, Pepe, never to ask."

"I'm sorry."

"Es nada."

"I wish you didn't have to fight monsters."

The dog walked over and sniffed El Matacerdos's boot, unsure if it was safe to be close to the man.

"He is getting big, not a puppy anymore."

"Are you staying with us again?"

"No, not this time."

The boy moaned in disapproval, but El Matacerdos shushed him.

"Next time, when I come back, I'll meet you in Hermosillo for *raspados.* But I have to go. I just wanted to see you. It's been too long."

"It has, Papa."

"Now, go back inside. The dog could use some shade. He is thirsty."

The boy did as he was instructed, and the dog followed him into the house.

El Matacerdos turned and went back to his car. He got in, retrieved the gun from the glove box, and put it in his holster. As he turned the car around to head down the hill, he saw his son step out the front door of the house and into the street. He drove off, and soon the house disappeared into the mix of history on the hilltop.

He drove north toward the monsters to be slain in Nuevo Negaldo.

60

Roberto had been born in the US and had spent his first years of life in El Paso, but he was Mexican at heart and the land south of the border was where he felt at home. His mother had loved him, still loved him, and he would do anything to protect her.

But as for him, he would not run. He would not leave.

She had worked to provide him a home his whole life. His father had disappeared while Roberto was still in utero. From the beginning it had just been the two of them. He was left to his own devices most of the time, and when they moved across the border to Nuevo Negaldo to take care of his grandmother, he had been left alone most days while his mother earned a paycheck.

Soon, he had found new people who wanted to treat him like family.

"Hey, kid," a voice had yelled to him one

m whistling at the Escalade th.
rived in. In the back, Adan wa.
table with a large stack of bills in
im, a pistol on the counter, and
en lying inebriated on a couch in
.

!" he said.

Roberto said. "I got some trouble
o."

s it?"

re, follow me."

tood, grabbed the pistol, and
nto his back. He followed Roberto
e garage. Adan's eyes lit up in
en he saw the truck. He knew
was instantly.

, no, no . . . ," Adan said, the re-
that Roberto just started a war
Cartel slowly washing over his face.
ou a present," Roberto said, toss-
ys to Adan.

afternoon.

"Yes?"

"Come over here."

Roberto crossed from the vacant lot where he had been kicking an old soccer ball against the wall of a cinder-block building. There were three men — boys most likely, but to Roberto they seemed so old — leaning against a rusted sedan, their pants hung low, white tank tops that were as spotless as the robes of the altar boys at church. They had ink up and down their arms in designs that were so complex that Roberto had to cross his eyes to make them out.

"Look at him, Adan, he's so small," one of the men said.

"Shut it, Chavez," Adan said before turning his eyes on Roberto. He was clearly the leader of this small group. "You like football, little muchacho?"

Roberto nodded his head.

"That ball . . . it's not really that good, is it? It's older than Chavez."

Roberto found himself trying to shield his ball from their eyes, suddenly ashamed by the apparent sign of poverty it showed to the world.

"Here, I got something for you," Adan said. He reached into the car and pulled out a brand-new Adidas soccer ball. It was colored red, green, and white. Roberto's eyes widened. He dropped his tattered old ball and took the new one in his hands. He didn't know what to say.

"Go on," Adan said, "try it out."

Roberto turned and dribbled the ball back to the lot. After kicking it around, he turned back to the street, but the men were gone. At home that night, he hid the new ball under the bed. He didn't know what his mother would say about it, and he didn't want to run the risk of having her make him give it back.

It seemed so benign at the time, but now as Roberto cruised through the streets of Nuevo Negaldo in the shot-up Cartel SUV, the passenger seat covered in blood, his mind went back to that moment. That was the moment he had decided on this life. He had sold his future for a soccer ball.

Adan returned a week later with a jersey for him, and he could have it if he could do a little job for him. It had been small favors to start, no big deal. Running messages, keeping track of strange people walking through the neighborhood. Roberto loved doing things for Adan.

Soon, the jobs started to get bigger, more dangerous. But what could he do? Adan was his friend, had provided such nice things.

And that was how he [...] Los Diablos. It was a [...] life, and it had broken [...]

When she came hom[...] greased by the fryer at [...] stained, and he was si[...] a new set of duds tha[...] uniform, she almost [...] furious and he had n[...] and headed to Adan's [...]

"Go home, 'Berto," [...] tor had company ar[...] wanted was a kid aro[...] morrow."

Roberto slunk ba[...] through the door, and [...] ing at the table. He d[...] inched toward the ba[...] into bed.

How many nights h[...]

And now he had de[...] had worked for here [...] fix this, not for himse[...] to keep her safe, and [...] for her to come hom[...]

He would go see A[...]

Roberto pulled the [...] into a garage. Two [...] behind him. He ste[...] and walked to the [...]

behind[...] he had [...] sitting [...] front [...] two wo[...] the co[...]

" 'Be[...] "Ada[...] on me,[...] "Wha[...] "Out [...] Adan [...] tucked [...] out to [...] shock [...] whose i[...] "No, [...] alizatio[...] with the [...] "I got [...] ing the [...]

61

Adan stood staring at the SUV in his garage and then started yelling at several men standing around in grease monkey suits.

"Strip it down. All of it," Adan said. "Now!"

The men got moving. They each grabbed tools to start tearing the vehicle apart and chopping it down into what would hopefully be smaller, untraceable parts. Adan then turned to Roberto, grabbed him by the arm, and dragged him back into his office. He told the women to leave and threw Roberto down into a chair.

"Is this why they wanted you?" Adan asked. "Is this why I have Salazar's men calling me asking about you?"

"No. This crew showed up at my house."

"Where's Miguel?"

"Miguel is dead."

Adan looked confused and dumbfounded, but then regained his composure. "What?"

Roberto told him the story, about how they found Felipe strung up in front of the church, how they had driven out to the migrant shelter, how Arturio and Vicente had shown up, the gunfight, and how Miguel had died.

"Two? You had two gunfights today?"

Roberto nodded. His eyes steely with bravado, just as he had learned from Adan.

"Why are they after you?"

Roberto didn't say a word. Adan pulled out his pistol and aimed it at Roberto's chest.

"Tell me, pendejo! Salazar is going to be coming down on everyone because of you, so you better tell me right now why I shouldn't just kill you myself. You ran that hit job with Miguel, what happened?"

"We picked up two guys. We drove them out of town and shot them."

"They anyone to us?"

"One was to me."

"Who?"

"Tyler Kazmierski."

Adan's gun hand started to shake as the frustration built up inside of him. He knew the story. He had heard how Tyler had taken a shank for Roberto back in the jail. It was why Adan agreed to give the gringo a chance, but he had never been 100 percent on board. Tyler was North American, for one thing.

"You didn't kill him, did you?" Adan said.

Roberto shook his head as he stared down the barrel of Adan's pistol. Soon he saw the gun lower and he could feel the cramping in his guts loosen. Adan turned and walked over to the far wall and looked out the window that opened out to the junk lot behind the building. The wire mesh covering over the glass gave the room a vague prison vibe. Roberto had known Adan long enough not to interrupt him while he was thinking. Either Adan would turn around and shoot him, or he would turn around and tell him what to do. Either option was a probability, and Roberto waited for that deciding moment to find out which it was going to be. He saw Adan's shoulders slump and his body turn.

"You put us in a bad spot, bro," Adan said. "The plaza is heating up. Word is that Salazar is getting squeezed by El Aguila. And Juarez is looking at taking over Nuevo Negaldo. El Aguila isn't going to let that happen. Salazar will either have to clear them out, or he'll get replaced. This business with Tyler, it just makes Salazar look weaker. That's where we might have a break."

Roberto listened. Adan went on with his stream of consciousness.

"Tyler knows where he dumped that load. That missing load. He stole it. You know it, and I know it. Salazar knows it. But if we get our hands on it, we can probably use it to leverage our way out of this. Either that, or we are going to have to go to war with Salazar, which puts us on the side of Juarez. But Juarez ain't going to take the plaza, ain't no way."

"So what do we do?"

"We find Tyler. We find that load. And we get it back to El Aguila. It will show that we are on his side. Then we hope that Salazar gets replaced. Either way, he's gunning for us."

"Tyler is already *norte.*"

Adan turned back to the window and let out a long exhale.

"Then we're all dead men."

62

Camilla did not know what to do but cry.

Her brother was dead.

Her son had told her to stay out of Nuevo Negaldo or she might be next.

Her hope of Roberto being redeemed was dashed.

She wept for him, for them all, like La Llorona weeping for her drowned children.

She could only imagine by what method Felipe had been killed. She knew the creative streak the Cartel had for killing people. She did not ask Roberto how it happened. She wanted to remember Felipe as she did — smiling, wearing his clerical collar and black shirt, his white cowboy hat pulled low over his brow. His dark eyes displaying a warmth that was all but absent in many of the men in town.

And now her son was lost too. She could tell it in his voice, by his words. He was scared. No, he would never admit it. His cholo façade always told the world not to mess with him, that he was one to stay clear of, to "back away from or you'll get cut, pendejos," but it never worked on her. She still saw the baby, the toddler, the inquisitive boy that Roberto used to be whenever he looked at her.

What was going to happen to him?

Roberto had told her to go to Deming. He pleaded and begged her to do so, as if he already knew that she would not listen to him. How could she leave him on his own at a time like this? How could she just abandon him when he was obviously in such desperate need of help? She would not leave, had no intention of leaving, but she would not go home tonight. That much she would listen to.

It had grown dark as she sat in the back room at La Casa de Irma, her eyes dry for the time being, the customers all gone for the night. She locked up the building and went to her car. Next to it was the truck of the American who went to Mexico to help his son. A parent much like her. Exactly like her. Where was he now? Was he dead too?

She had no emotion left for him. For Edward. He seemed like a good guy. A good man. But his name and his son's name were now a poison in her mind. She thought that

Roberto was doing an act of mercy for Tyler, but in the end it had cost the life of those she loved. She loved her family and it was hard for her to feel like this stranger's boy was worth it.

Camilla went to the truck and opened the door. Above the visor on the passenger side, she grabbed the motel key that she had stashed there and put it in her pocket. She closed the door, got in her car, and drove across the street. She parked in the space in front of the room Edward had rented and went inside. Since she couldn't go home, she thought she might as well use this spot. It was free, and it would let her stay minutes away from Roberto if he called and needed her.

The room was dark and she went to the sink and turned on the light. In the mirror she saw herself. It seemed like she had aged since the morning. Her bloodshot eyes could produce no more tears. They would in time, but now she was numb.

Camilla washed her face, dried off with a towel, and turned out the light. She made her way to the bed and lay down on the bedspread. The stillness of the room was suffocating. Somewhere a few miles south, her son was running, hiding, fighting. Who knew what he was doing? The uncertainty gripped her stomach, her womb aching to know that the child who had resided there so many years ago was safe and sound somewhere across the border.

Her pain and anxiety ebbed and flowed through the night, and just as sleep was attempting to overtake her exhausted mind, there was a knock on the door. She lay silent, her heart beating fast, her mind racing to think of who it could possibly be.

Roberto, it had to be Roberto. He had crossed over and seen her car in the parking lot. It had to be him.

Another knock on the door.

She rose from the bed and went to the door, opening it without reservation.

But it wasn't her son.

"Hello, Mrs. Ibanez, strange to see you here," Agent Lomas said as he pushed himself into the room and slammed the door behind him.

63

Camilla was told to sit in the chair that Lomas pulled out from the dilapidated desk in the room. She did so without argument as she kept her eyes on the agent. He searched the room, under the bed, in the bathroom. There was no one else here. He walked over and locked the door, then turned to her. She could feel her heart beating in her throat, not knowing what this man was going to do.

"Where is he?"

"Who?" she said.

"Don't make this hard on yourself."

"I don't know."

"What?"

"I don't know where he is."

"So," Lomas said, "are you and Kazmierski living together now?"

"What? No."

"Then why are you in his room?"

"I was too tired to drive home," she lied.

"I knew he had this room and he was not using it."

"And how did you know he wasn't using it?"

Camilla didn't answer. Already Lomas had made her doubt her ability to cover her actions.

"Where did you leave him yesterday?"

"I don't know."

"Yes, you do. You drove him over to a hostel and dropped him off. Who told you to do that?"

Again, Camilla held her tongue. She was not good at lying, even less so when her pulse was pounding in her ears as she wondered if she would ever make it out of this room.

Lomas took off his coat, threw it on the bed, and rolled up his sleeves. She could see that he was sweating, even though the air that night was unseasonably cool. He was nervous, but not of her. Something else was on his mind.

"This can go several different ways," Lomas said. "I can take you in for obstruction, but that would just be the start. Aiding and abetting. Conspiracy. You'd spend a long time in a cell somewhere where nobody will know where to look for you. It really isn't that hard. Trust me.

"Or, I can take you across the line and drop you in the plaza. Roberto has been busy today. You'd be a welcome token for Salazar to use to get him to show himself."

"What do you mean?" she said. She didn't want to know, but the words came out of her mouth before she could stop herself.

"Roberto has killed several Cartel sicarios, all in one day."

Camilla shook her head, not wanting to believe what Lomas was saying.

"Yes," he said. "There is a bounty on his head so large that all of Nuevo Negaldo will be looking for him. He's gone to ground somewhere, but I'm sure knowing that you were in the hands of Salazar would make him show himself."

"Is that why they killed Felipe?" she shouted. "Is that why they killed my brother?"

"See, you do know what's going on, don't you."

The tears started welling up in the corners of her eyes again, her world crashing in around her. Lomas walked over to the sink, filled a glass with water, and brought it over to her. He changed his tone.

"I don't care about Roberto. He can stay hiding until the end of time. I'm sorry for your brother . . . this . . . priest. We are dealing with savages. I'll even go so far as saying that your son was justified in taking revenge for his uncle. It wasn't smart, but I can understand. But now, for you, just tell me what I need to know and you can rest assured that your part in this is over. Okay?"

Camilla sipped the water, wiped her eyes, and gave a subtle nod.

"Now, Ed Kazmierski came down here, met with you, and you told him to go to Nuevo Negaldo. Why?"

"To meet with Felipe."

"The priest?"

"Yes."

"Why did you tell him to do that?"

Camilla breathed in and out. She felt like she was betraying her son, betraying Felipe. She didn't know what the right thing was to do.

"Roberto told me to," she said.

"And why would Roberto tell you to do that?"

"Because Felipe had something."

"Had what?"

Camilla's lip quivered. The answer was the last thing she had left. While she retained it, she had leverage. Once spoken, she was at the mercy of Lomas, and she had no idea what level of mercy he might offer. She knew the stories, had read the papers, the news. The bodies found in the desert, in the streets, in burning barrels on the ridges overlooking the city. The guilty, dead and disposed of, all while the citizens ignored the smoking pyres. She would become one of the shunned and her heart ached. She wanted Roberto to be here with her, to hold on to him, to have him protect her through this fear.

"What did Felipe have?"

What did she owe to this American? Who was he to her? Why should she trade her life to protect him from Agent Lomas, the Cartel, the men that butchered Felipe? He was the cause of this. If not him, his son. Tyler Kazmierski.

"You will not harm Roberto?" she asked faintly.

"I have no control over that. Roberto is in Mexico, and I am here. But I promise you that I will not harm you."

She swallowed hard.

"Felipe had . . . Edward's son. Tyler," she said.

Lomas's eyes widened.

"You're sure?" he asked.

She nodded again.

"And Roberto set it up?"

"Yes."

■ ■ ■ ■

Lomas paced around the room and put the pieces of what he knew together. Ed went to the church to meet up with Tyler. But they didn't cross over the border. So they were either still at the church or . . .

But if they were at the church, Salazar's men would have found them when they killed the priest. No, they had gotten out somehow. They were going to cross over some other way. Roberto was in two gunfights that day, one outside his mother's house in Nuevo Negaldo. Odds were that they would not have stayed in the city. The first fight, however, was at a migrant camp. It was empty by the time more men had arrived and reported back the carnage. There were no dead gringos in the place.

They were hoofing it through the desert.

He pulled out his phone, opened Google maps, and looked at the area.

"So," he said to himself, "they are taking the long way home."

By now, they would be on his side of the wire. Both of them. And one of them had in his possession the knowledge of where the missing load was. It was served up for him better than he could have imagined. It was time to make his score.

Lomas walked over and grabbed Camilla by the arm and forced her to her feet.

"Get up," he said, "we're going for a ride."

64

The water was running low and what was left was hoarded like gold.

The group was still together. No one had fallen off.

It was the small hours of the night and the men were walking north under the stars like the Magi. Ed brought up the rear of the moving column, his eyes fixed on Tyler's back, his on the man before him, and so on, with Julio leading the procession. They walked a trail that had been beaten out of the landscape by thousands of feet before them, their own steps adding to the compacting effort of migration. The path curved down a dry arroyo and followed a ridgeline for a mile, weaving snakelike through the country. The men crested the ridge and plodded on.

The darkness was overpowering and the nocturnal sounds of the desert expanse called out to them with each step. Ed's legs were burning, his quads tightening, the first indication of a blister was forming on the arch of his foot. He wondered as to the foolishness of this journey. He was in no shape to be hiking through the night. His body had gotten old without his notice, had aged and atrophied.

Tyler was struggling too. Even in the dark his pallor stood out, his gait was slouched.

"You alright?" Ed whispered.

Tyler grunted. He hadn't said more than a few words since they had talked with the Guatemalans.

"Do you know where we are?" Ed said.

"No."

"Okay."

Ed looked up. There was nothing out here. No signs, no lights, nothing to tell them where Mexico ended and America started. Before him, endless, uninterrupted nature.

They walked on, the rocks beneath his feet crunching with each footfall.

He adjusted the packs, the one on his back, the other slung on his chest. He was sweating more than he had in a long time. To keep his mind off his own pain, he tried to concentrate on the swaying cadence of Tyler's motion before him.

Like a gaunt, skeletal metronome.

His mind cleared with a slow epiphany.

311

For too long he had viewed Tyler's place in his life as if it were a celestial body moving in orbit around its host star. He being fixed in place, his son moved by the natural order, brought into being by his parents. To Ed, Tyler was simply navigating a path set down before the dawn of time, an adornment to Ed's life. But Tyler was more than that, had always been more than that. Ed was too ignorant to see that his son was, in fact, a world unto his own.

What kind of father was he?

Two steps in front of him was a grown man. His shoulders weakened by the patched gunshot wound and the loss of blood and energy. His body lean from years of self-abuse. But all the while his midnight ambulation through that desolate patch of country showed that he was built for this new world. He was a man who had passed through fire. And though his route in life had been marked by bad decisions, Ed watched Tyler guide his walk with purpose and a deftness of skill.

What had his son seen?

What had he experienced in life that was so far removed from Ed's own story? His son looked on the world through a glass tinted with the roughest abrasions, and Ed, for the first time he could remember, wanted to know what that view looked like.

He wanted to know his son.

He wanted to know why he did the things he had done. Why he wandered. Why he lusted after the drugs he put in his veins, why he would put himself in such straits as these. What went through his son's mind when he thought of the future? Did he think of such things?

And then Ed considered the most jarring notion. Did he love Tyler? Had he ever really loved him?

A rock caught his foot and he stumbled. The ground came up fast and his face smashed against the hardpan. The pack on his front side smashed against his ribs and took the breath out of him. Tyler turned and helped him back to his feet without saying a word.

They walked on.

His mind went back to his thoughts.

When his wife had left, he shut down. There was no getting around that fact. He didn't really know how to take care of his boy. He knew how to pay the bills, how to make sure that Tyler had a place to sleep and that the chores were done, but that was about it. Their relationship was mechanical. It was simply mathematics with no art. And so when Tyler started getting into trouble, the equation became unbalanced and Ed found himself no longer interested in trying to solve it.

He told himself at the time that he was giving tough love, teaching resiliency, teaching the boy that when it came to correcting mistakes, it was up to him and him alone to fix them.

But in reality he had taught Tyler that he wasn't worth the effort.

Was that true? Was Tyler really that much of a burden after his wife left, or had the abandonment and resentment just overtaken him so much that all he could do was make sure that nothing else ever touched his heart again, even to the point of pushing away his own boy?

A child is so much more than a derivative of a parent's baser traits, more than a collection of faults passed down that a father is afraid will expose parts of himself to the world. Every mistake that Tyler had made was an affront to Ed's sense of pride, as if each act of the son deducted from the character of the father. But now, on this trail, Ed saw, as with new eyes, the man before him.

Not an extension of himself that caused pain to the whole, but an independent being as he himself knew he was.

His son.

Ed thought of his own father, how it was easy to believe that his old man had come into existence at the moment of his first memory, that his father had not lived before Ed was in the world to observe it. How little he had cared for his own father's instruction. The same way that Tyler had disregarded his advice.

They were alike, father and son, but not the same, and this separation of identity in Ed's thoughts could not have happened anywhere else but on this journey through the desert.

Tyler turned around again to make sure his father was still on his feet.

They all walked on.

65

Crossing into the States was less dramatic than what Ed had expected. Julio held down two lines of barbed wire while the men stepped over one by one. They were home. Unlike their traveling companions, the anxiety for Ed and Tyler diminished with each additional step.

The group came to a stop and the men took the opportunity to sit down. Julio walked ahead and pulled something out of his pocket.

"What's he doing?" Edward asked.

"Burner phone," Tyler said.

"What's that?"

Tyler still wasn't that interested in talking, but he relented. "There are lookouts on these hills watching for Border Patrol. They're letting him know where to go."

"Lookouts?"

"Yeah. Guys camped out on the peaks.

They'll stay up there for days directing traffic."

Edward kept his eyes on the coyote. Julio pocketed the phone, walked back to the group, and everyone got back on their feet. They then set off again. Julio led them to a declivity that fell away into a steep valley, then turned north, and navigated along a dry wash before coming out the other side. They were making their way to a mountain spire isolated on the plain, its huge bulk silhouetted in the twilight sky. They soon found themselves ascending a narrow path to an opening framed by old timbers barely the height of the shortest in the group.

"An old silver mine," Tyler said before his father could ask.

They ventured in single file and followed the course of the mine several hundred feet, then one by one each of them descended a ladder in the dark. Edward followed his son down, Luis and Juan bringing up the rear. The smell of all the men soon turned the tunnel rancid.

Once down the ladder, they all journeyed on into the mountain, hunched over like trolls. Every muscle of Ed's body was burning, and he was convinced his back was about to seize and paralyze him. But before he lay down and quit, he could feel fresh air blowing down the tunnel. They emerged on the other side of the rock and stood, each stretching and breathing in clean oxygen.

Julio had been the first through the cave, and when Ed emerged, he saw that the coyote was on the phone again.

"What now?" Ed asked.

"The highway. You can barely make it out over there. We have to wait here until the pickup time."

"Do you think he's telling someone about us?"

"Absolutely," Tyler said calmly.

"And . . ."

"We're on the US side, so we have that going for us. We'll make a break for it at some point."

"What if who he is talking to comes for us first?"

"Too risky. I figure either Julio tries to take us here on his own and march us back to Mexico, or he'll wait until we hit the highway where he'll have backup. I bet he doesn't have the guts to try to make a move out here on his own."

"And if he does?"

"Like I said, I'll take care of it."

Ed nodded. It wasn't just youthful or thuggish bravado coming from Tyler. It was reserved confidence.

Julio looked back at him, the phone still on his ear, the same impish smirk on his face.

They waited.

An hour or more had passed when Julio looked at his watch and then forced everyone up. The group made its way down the mountain and double-timed it toward the highway. Their bodies burning, their muscles exhausted, each man running toward his destiny.

On and on through the endless desert.

The lights of the road running perpendicular to their course came into view, the headlights of sporadic vehicles crisscrossing the landscape. The troop kept moving, relief and smiles on the Guatemalans' faces as they looked back at Edward and were surprised that he didn't seem to share their enthusiasm. Ed looked to Tyler to see what they were going to do.

The group stopped twenty yards from the road and waited behind a berm topped with brush.

"What now?" Ed whispered.

Tyler shook his head.

They all sat.

Soon, a van pulled up from the west and stopped abruptly. With a grunt, Julio directed the migrants toward it. Each man ran for the vehicle as if afraid there wouldn't be enough room for them all. They filed in, but when Tyler and Ed arrived, Julio pulled out a handgun from the passenger window and stepped between them.

He yelled something in Spanish.

"Get in the van, Dad," Tyler said.

"What?"

"Get in the van."

"What's happening?"

Julio spewed more talk.

"Looks like I'm not going," Tyler said, his hands raised as Julio pointed the gun at him. "You go, Dad. Get out of here."

And so, this was it.

The moment in life that sets the trajectory for the rest of your days. Most people only recognize it in hindsight. In memory. But for Ed, this moment rushed upon him like a desert wind, blasting his thoughts and exposing his life, past and future, to the decision he had to make.

"No . . . ," Ed said under his breath.

Julio turned to him, the gun raised, more angry words.

"Dad!" Tyler yelled.

"No," Ed said louder, the tremor in his voice still noticeable. He drew a breath, and with it came a voice he'd never heard from himself. A voice which carried the weight of so many silences, places when he should have spoken up and didn't.

The pistol was now aimed at his forehead. His legs were shaking and Ed thought they would give out at any moment.

"I'm not leaving!"

He would die with Tyler knowing that his father did not abandon him.

The driver in the van started shouting. The migrants already in the van started in too. They couldn't wait out here in the open. Julio yelled back, the cacophony of foreign voices rising in the air.

"Dad!"

"I'm not leaving, I'm not leaving! I'm never leaving!"

Suddenly the driver hit the gas and the van took off down the highway, leaving the coyote and the two gringos awash in its taillights.

66

Tyler sat down in the dirt, grabbing Ed's arm on the way down.

"Sit down, Dad," Tyler said.

Ed's energy was spent, but he was resolved. "What's he going to do?"

"I don't know."

Julio yelled again, and Ed didn't need a translator to understand that the coyote wanted them to shut up. Julio pulled his cell phone out, called a number, said a few words, and then put it back. He backed up a couple paces and then sat down himself, keeping the gun trained on them.

Daylight came upon them all and the shadows moved across the land. Their water was gone.

They waited.

A car would appear in the distance and then fly by their position and be gone. The distant mountains became lost in a haze, shaded by nothing more than too much atmosphere. After a couple hours, his skin was burning. It felt like Ed had never been so close to the sun before.

From the east a car approached quickly. While a little more than a quarter mile away, it slowed dramatically and started to creep down the blacktop. Julio's phone vibrated. He stood up and backed away from Ed and Tyler toward the road.

The car came to a stop when Julio waved it down and the door opened.

A man stepped onto the road.

"Ed! Tyler?" the man yelled. It was Agent Lomas.

Ed perked up when he heard his name.

"Here!" Ed yelled from the back side of the embankment. He stood and walked over to the road. He started to feel a sense of relief, like this whole ordeal was coming to an end. "You have no idea how happy I am to see you, I thought —"

Lomas raised his gun where they could see it.

"On your knees, Ed," Lomas said. "Tyler! I know you're out there. Get over here next to your dad."

After what seemed like forever, Tyler emerged from hiding and took his place on his knees next to Ed. Lomas holstered his gun and from his pocket took out some zip ties and cuffed Tyler. Then he did the same to Ed.

"I told you, Ed, you should have told me what was going on."

Ed didn't say anything.

"You go south, start a shooting gallery from what I heard, bodies piling up all over the place in Nuevo Negaldo, and then here you are sneaking through the desert?" Lomas said. He walked over to Julio, and spoke to him. Ed watched as Julio pulled the pistol from his waistband and handed it to Lomas. The agent looked it over and grunted.

"This could have gone so much different if you had just talked to me, Ed. What were you thinking? I mean, really. Look at him." Lomas pointed at Tyler. "He's a loser. Why would you put yourself in this position for him? It doesn't make any sense. Now it's gotten way too complicated."

Lomas raised Julio's gun, and before Ed's mind could contemplate what was happening, the agent fired, putting a bullet right between Julio's eyes. Ed's stomach dropped and he dry heaved.

Lomas walked behind Ed and Tyler. Ed had no idea if this was his last moment on earth when a canvas bag went over his head and was cinched at the neck. Lomas lifted him to his feet and guided him to the car.

Ed was put in the back seat and the door was closed.

He waited there in the dark. He tried to calm his breathing as he listened for what he was sure to be the gunshot that would kill his son. Agent Lomas had killed the unarmed smuggler without even batting an eye. Why would he be any more reserved with them? The opening of the car door across from him eased his nerves as he felt Tyler being pushed in beside him. The door closed and they were alone in the car.

"You okay, Dad?"

"Yes."

"You sure."

Ed grunted.

"You know this guy?"

"Lomas. His name is Lomas. FBI, or DEA, or something. He was asking me questions about you the past several days. Wondering if I knew where you were."

"When was the last time you saw him?"

"The night Camilla drove me to Mexico."

Ed felt what must have been Tyler kicking the seat in front of him.

"He's Cartel."

"What?"

"Lomas . . . must be Cartel or paid off by Salazar."

"That means?"

Ed heard Tyler sigh, then the sound of the driver's door opening and Lomas getting in the car. He put it in drive and they felt the motion of the vehicle turning around and heading back in the direction from which it had come.

Behind them, Julio's body lay on the road, a pistol tossed beside him, and his vacant eyes staring up at the blistering sun.

67

They rode with their heads covered in the back seat of the car. Edward had naïvely started asking questions, and Lomas repeatedly told him to shut up. It wasn't until their captor stopped the car, opened Ed's door, and pistol-whipped him that the idea to keep his mouth shut finally took hold.

They were driven for what seemed like hours. The vehicle kept a straight course, the smooth road under them giving no indication how fast they were moving. Eventually the car slowed, made a hard right, and then accelerated again.

"Get down," Lomas said.

"Why?" Ed asked.

This time Lomas didn't stop the car to bust Ed in the head.

"I said get down."

Several minutes passed and they pulled into an area with the sounds of commotion all around the car. They came to a stop and

Ed could hear voices.

Two men, Lomas one of them, argued back and forth in Spanish. Tyler's door opened, Ed heard a few laughs from another man who must have been standing close by, and then the door was shut again.

The car began to accelerate and soon they were zigzagging through city streets.

"We are back," Tyler whispered. His voice was close to Ed's ear.

"Where?"

"Nuevo Negaldo."

"What?"

"He's brought us back."

"That's right," Lomas said, "I gave you a chance. You could have told me where the load was. We could have made a deal."

"You would have killed us," Tyler said.

"You're dead anyway. Salazar isn't going to make the same mistake again. Roberto won't be the one pulling the trigger this time."

"Let my dad go. This ain't his show," Tyler said.

"He's not leaving."

"Let him go!" Tyler screamed.

Ed heard kicking, as if Tyler had brought his legs up and was attempting to bust the driver's seat in front of him. The car swerved and then Lomas applied the brakes hard.

The vehicle came to a screeching halt, Ed's forward momentum carrying him into the seat in front of him, smashing his face. Blinding pain shot through his nose.

Lomas stepped out of the car and opened Tyler's door. Ed could hear blows being dealt out viciously, his son holding his tongue with each punch.

"Stop it!" Ed yelled. "Stop!" The pain in his face made his voice weak.

The beating stopped after Lomas put in one last hard hit for good measure. The door was shut, Lomas climbed back in the driver's seat, and they were on their way again. Tyler slumped to his side, his weight collapsing on Ed's shoulder.

"You going to be okay?" Ed whispered.

Tyler grunted, and Ed could feel his son nod slightly.

They rode like this for several minutes, turning left and right, navigating through the streets of Nuevo Negaldo, until they started to rise up a hill. Tyler mumbled something inaudible.

"What?" Ed asked.

"Salazar's place. We're here."

"He's right," Lomas said.

Ed could hear a voice from what sounded like a fast-food speaker, then the noise of a large iron gate opening, and the car moved on. Lomas brought the car to a stop, the doors opened, and several hands grabbed at Ed. He was lifted out of the car and practically dragged away, his toes barely reaching the ground. He was carried up stone steps, and suddenly air conditioning hit his body full force as he was ushered along.

He was in a house, the footsteps of his captors echoing in what sounded like a large stone entryway. On and on until eventually they moved him down a stairway. Vertigo started to overtake his mind as down and down they went. He breathed hard against the hood.

Down and down they went. Ed thought he would suffocate. He couldn't get enough air. Panic.

Finally the floor leveled out and his guards forced him to sit in a chair. The zip ties on his wrists were cut, but before he could stretch his muscles, his arms and ankles were taped down to the chair. Once done, his captors left him and all was silent.

Ed sat, taped to a chair, a bag over his head, in what could only be the basement of a Cartel drug lord. The silence of the room was deafening. His own heart beat in his ears and sweat poured from his brow, leaching into the bag, causing a self-induced sensation of waterboarding with each breath.

He was scared. He was beyond all his comprehension of the notion of scared.

Then he heard something that sounded like the scuffing of a foot on a sandy floor. "Tyler? Tyler, is that you?"

"Ed?" a voice said back. It was feminine.

"Camilla?"

"Yes, it's me," she said.

"Where are you?"

"Over here."

It wasn't long until they realized they both were similarly constrained, hooded, and coming to grips that their futures were tied up in the actions of their wayward sons.

68

El Matacerdos arrived in Nuevo Negaldo as
the sun was reaching its zenith. It had been
years since he had been here, but the city
hadn't changed much. He had taken the
main road up from Hermosillo, stopping
overnight, and then looked for a motel on
the southern side of the city. Something
about the border made him uneasy. It had
always been that way, and so he kept his
distance. He had been sent to Juarez and
Nogales before but had never crossed over
into the US.

In Mexico, things made sense to him.

North of the border, not so much.

Satisfied with the motel's location, he paid
cash, then parked his car, pulled his duffel
out of the trunk, and went to his room. The
dry desert air seeped through the walls as
he placed his bag on the bed and searched
the small room. Once content that this
wasn't the day he was being set up for his

own execution, he barricaded the door and went in to take a shower.

The water poured over him and washed away the past several days of sins. Here as the steam rose and filled the room, his body stood still, but his mind kept moving on the roads he had traveled and the men he had killed. It was an endless highway of places and faces — angry men, crying men, men pleading for their lives. They haunted his mind, but none so much as those at peace to allow him to do what he had been commissioned to do.

There had only been a few, those who were calm, the fatalists. The spiritual perhaps. In his business there were not many, but there were some.

Salazar was not one of those men.

El Matacerdos knew Salazar from way back. He had watched his rise in the Cartel with befuddled amusement. From the very beginning it was apparent to him Salazar would end up shot for ineptitude, but he had the luck of being born into a distant branch of El Aguila's family. When he was given the plaza in Nuevo Negaldo, word was that one of the other cartels would move against him as soon as he arrived.

His weakness as a capo had been exposed in a different way, however. He was losing shipments apparently. And that was one thing El Aguila could not tolerate. Not even from his own family.

El Matacerdos stepped out of the shower, dried off, wrapped the towel around himself, and sat on the bed. From the duffel he pulled out a clean set of clothes, dark jeans and a T-shirt. He got dressed and then inspected his weapons. He had two pistols. Each the same. Redundancy in the event that one should malfunction, which was unlikely since they were meticulously maintained.

He put them in the shoulder holsters, then put his jacket on over top.

Salazar's place was a short drive away. He would be leaving as soon as the job was done, but his eyes were heavy from the long drive and the effects of the shower. He lay down on the bed, his feet still on the floor, and stared at the ceiling until his eyes closed and he drifted to sleep. A fevered sleep with the faces of the long dead dancing in his brain.

There would be more faces added in a few hours, and the nightmares would grow and the devil's road would get longer, but for now, he rested with the ghosts of the past.

69

Roberto was starting to lose it. His mother had gone off the grid. He kept calling her phone but was always bounced to voicemail. He called his aunt up in Deming; his mother had not arrived. He heard that same message each time he called.

She had disappeared. More than likely she had not disappeared accidentally.

Everything in him wanted to cross the border and go to Hurtado to find her, to drive the route up to Deming and see if he could retrace her steps. But he was stuck here in Nuevo Negaldo.

His hands shook. He paced the room in the back of Adan's garage where he had been told to stay. After the course of the past several days, he would have thought his body would be on the point of collapsing, but out of some unknown reserve, his adrenaline kept on pumping.

Salazar's paid stooges at the border crossing would take him out if he tried to cross, and he wasn't about to go slumping across the wild to get up north like some lowlife bum. He was stuck, with a million watts of bottled-up energy and no place to exorcise it.

He pulled a cerveza from the mini fridge Adan kept stocked and tried to sit down on the couch. Then he stood and moved to the small counting table in the middle of the room. Back and forth he went, like a junkie on the street twerking on a bad hit.

Where was she?

He tried her phone again.

He should never have involved his uncle. He was a good man, the only truly good man he had known in his life. Now his uncle was dead. Miguel was dead. What if his mother was dead? What if Salazar had gone after her?

He got up and threw the empty bottle against the wall where it shattered like fireworks.

The door opened.

"You alright?"

"Where's Adan?" Roberto asked.

"He's coming. Five minutes."

The door closed.

Roberto wasn't being held prisoner, but he couldn't leave either. Adan had taken his gun, as he did to everyone coming into his shop. He wanted to be sure if there was ever an attempt of a coup that he would be the only one armed. Roberto going out onto the street without his firearm would be the equivalent of committing suicide. So all he could do was wait.

And wait some more.

Eventually, he could hear noise in the garage and the door opened. Adan walked in and shut it behind him. He then sat down at the table across from Roberto.

"You sure Miguel was dead?" Adan asked.

"Yes, positive."

"They found him this morning. Or at least parts of him over on Revolución Street. It is good to know he was dead before they butchered him."

Roberto's jaw tightened as he listened.

"Salazar's turning over every rock looking for you. He's squeezing everyone, even me. Wants to know where you are. Wants me to bring you in or to kill you myself."

"What are you going to do?"

Adan reached into his belt and pulled out Roberto's pistol. Roberto's breath stopped as he looked at the weapon from the other end. Instead of seeing a muzzle flash and eternal darkness, Adan laid it on the table and pushed it across. Roberto didn't know whether to pick it up or not.

"He's got your mom, bro."

Roberto's eyes lit up and he stood to his feet, his fists clenched, he needed something to punch.

"Where?"

"His place."

"You see her?"

"Yes."

"Alive?"

Adan nodded. "She looked okay. He hadn't roughed her up yet."

Roberto looked down at the pistol.

"Take it," Adan said, "you're going to need it."

He reached out, picked up the piece, and chambered a round.

"I'm not taking you in and I'm not killing you," Adan said, reclining back. "But I can't go with you. It's suicide. And if you don't know by now, I enjoy living. Enjoy living a lot. You've been a good soldier, Roberto. Wish you wouldn't have gone and screwed it up."

While Adan had been talking, Roberto's mind was already miles ahead, thinking how he was going to get into Salazar's place. It was a virtual fortress with armed men and a gated entrance. It wasn't a question of whether he was going in after his mother, but simply how he was going to go about doing it.

"I need to get in."

Adan stared back.

"Can you get me in? Anything, please, Adan."

Adan thought about it, and then conceded. "I can get you inside the gate. After that, I'm out. You wait for me to get back on the street before you start anything. If you get caught and say my name, I'll find anybody you've ever cared about and kill them all. You understand?"

Roberto nodded.

"You're as good as dead once you're inside."

"I know."

"But hey, you deserve a chance, right?" Adan grunted. "You've always done right by me."

"I've tried," Roberto said.

"This must be how you got roped in with this Tyler, huh? An impulsive, stupid decision like this."

"Yeah."

"Alright. Let's get this over with."

The two left the room, walked outside, and got into the back seat of a sedan with windows tinted as dark as midnight. Adan's

driver fired up the car and headed to Salazar's compound.

70

"Did you think you could steal from me?"

A fist crushed Tyler's abdomen and he would have doubled over on the ground except for the two large men holding him. His legs were like jelly and his flesh was bruising with each passing second.

"Do you think I'm an idiot?" Salazar said.

He punched him again, then took a step back. He motioned with his hand and one of the goons grabbed a chair and sat Tyler on it. Tyler's left eye was swollen, his nose was broken, his lip split. His head was held up by one of the men, who now grabbed him by the back of his hair.

Salazar pointed at Tyler's shoulder. "What is that?"

Salazar approached Tyler, ripped his shirt open, and saw the bandage on the gringo's shoulder. He grabbed at it and pulled it off. A bullet hole partially healed but now oozing from one of the previously thrown punches.

"So he *did* shoot you, eh?"

Salazar walked over to his desk, grabbed a silver letter opener from a drawer, and walked back.

"Hold him still," Salazar said to the men.

He pushed the letter opener into the hole on Tyler's back. Tyler tensed with pain, a scream echoing in his throat that could not find release past the hand which clasped his mouth shut. His eyes clenched, tears forming, the white-hot heat in his shoulder radiating through his body. Salazar forced the tool out the other side and stood up, admiring his work.

"Clean through. Amazing shot. What a waste. A gun hand like that could have made a fortune with me. But here, he wasted his talents on a pendejo like you."

Tyler convulsed. He wanted nothing more than the silver stick to be removed. He wanted this to end. But Salazar would not let it. He would drag this on for as long as he possibly could. Salazar went back to his desk, sat down, and took a cigar from the humidor on the desk. He lit it with great flair.

"Where is my shipment?"

Smoke from the cigar drifted through the room. Salazar's words entered Tyler's ears, but all he could think about was the searing fire in his shoulder.

"You tell me, and this all stops. I'll make it quick. I'll make it so they can bury you in one box, not three. That seems fair, doesn't it?"

Tyler was on the verge of blacking out. The blood from Tyler's lip dripped down his chin, his vision started swirling. Suddenly Salazar was standing before him again.

"Where is my shipment? Where did you dump it?"

Salazar put a finger on the letter opener, moving it up and down a little. Fresh pain shot through Tyler's shoulder.

"Where is it?" Salazar screamed.

Tyler's head flopped down, and as he lost consciousness, he heard Salazar give an order to one of the men behind him.

"Bring his father up here."

71

"Are you hurt?" Ed asked Camilla.

"No."

"What happened?"

She told him about how Roberto told her to go to Deming. How Agent Lomas had said he was arresting her, but instead of driving to El Paso, he drove her here.

"He did the same to us," Ed said.

"What are we going to do?"

"I have no idea."

He could hear a soft cry escape on her breath. There was no hope he could lend to her. This was the end. He knew enough of the world to know that they would not be leaving this house.

She spoke again, and the rhythm of her words was shaky, as if she was trying to portray confidence in the face of overwhelming terror.

"I would have liked to have met under different circumstances," she said.

"Maybe after all this is over," Ed said.

"Maybe," she said.

72

Adan's car pulled up to the gates. The driver rolled down his tinted window, and from the back seat, Adan yelled to the guard to open up. The guard stood from his post, his hand resting on the top of his machine gun. He stuck his head in the window.

"You back already, Adan?"

"Just open the gate, pendejo."

"What's going on?"

"Open the gate, or I'll shoot you right here."

The guard cracked a smile, flipped a switch, and the gates started to open. The driver brought the vehicle into the compound and backed in against a manicured shrub that took more water than it was worth to keep alive.

"Alright, we're in," Adan said.

Roberto rubbed his hands on his pants. No matter how hard he tried, he couldn't keep the sweat off them. He stared out into the compound. Salazar's hacienda was up the steps to his right. To his left, he could see out over the plain below, across Nuevo Negaldo and on into the United States.

"Any idea how many men he has in there?" Roberto asked.

"No idea. I would assume a lot."

"And where did you see my mother?"

"They had just brought her in through the door when we were leaving. I have no idea where they would have put her."

"So I just go through the front door and start searching."

Adan thought about it. His face showed the sign of a man wrestling against common sense. "You won't make it through the front door," Adan said, "and if you do, I doubt you'd make it to the second floor."

"I'm going anyway."

Roberto checked his weapon again for the hundredth time, his nerves getting the best of him. His adrenaline was pumping, the fight-or-flight portion of his brain stuck in neutral and overheating. Adan reached over and grabbed his arm.

"Hold up. I got an idea," Adan said. "Give me your gun."

"Why should I trust you?" Roberto asked.

"If you don't by now, then there is no

hope for you. They'll search you. Me they trust."

Roberto relented and handed over his weapon. Adan tucked it into his jacket.

"Just keep your mouth shut. You got me?"

Roberto nodded.

Adan tapped the driver on the shoulder and said, "Let's go, amigo." They exited the car and Adan motioned for Roberto to follow. Walking up to the house in broad daylight seemed foolish, but he followed Adan's commands.

They walked up the stone steps to the mansion's front door, and it opened as they approached. The guard on the inside spoke to Adan and nodded to the driver. He knew them. He did not know Roberto, and as anticipated, Roberto was frisked before they were allowed to pass.

Inside, it felt more like a hotel than a house, and there were several people milling about. Adan went toward a quiet spot and pulled Roberto in close. He gave Roberto his gun back and then held out his hand to the driver, who produced a suppressor from his pocket. Adan gave it to Roberto.

"Find a spot in here to lay low. Give me an hour to be gone, you got me?"

Roberto nodded.

"I'm serious, bro. An hour. I have no doubt you're not going to make it out, but good luck. If you do make it out . . . never mind, you won't. This is it for us. Too much heat is going to come down. It ain't going to come down on me, you hear?"

Roberto nodded as Adan slapped him on the shoulder, looked into his eyes, and departed with the driver. Roberto followed a man in a pressed linen suit and then ducked into a side room that was empty. He turned and watched as Adan left through the front door and was gone.

From the opposite end of the building, emerging from an archway that led to a lower level, two men appeared with a third in tow. The man between them was hooded and being practically dragged up to the second level of the hacienda.

Roberto was in the belly of the beast. Somewhere in this maze of a house was his mother. She just had to hold tight until the shooting began.

73

They brought Edward up from the basement. As they did so, he tried to give a parting grunt to Camilla, who was equally blind to what was happening, and he heard her Spanish tongue reciting something at his departure. Her voice was angelic, a holy psalm as he was led through the valley of death. His captors forced him up the stairs, his feet tripping over themselves. From the back of a truck, to the desert walk, to being bound in Salazar's mansion, his body was losing all muscle strength. Even if they cut him loose now, he was sure that he wouldn't have the strength or stamina to run a hundred feet. His throat was dry, and all he could think about, apart from whether he would be dead soon, was how thirsty he was.

The stairs were never-ending, and by the time they were halfway up, the men were carrying him, his feet dragging on the steps, up and up.

Finally, the stairs stopped, and he sensed that he was brought into a room. Ed could smell cigar smoke, and the air, which was warmer and thicker than in the basement, wrapped around his body.

Another chair. More duct tape. Once he was secured, the sack came off his head.

Across from him, similarly tied down in a seat, was Tyler. His son. The catalyst for this grand adventure. Tyler looked as if he had been hit by a truck. His face was swelling up on the left side, he sat slumped down, his shoulder exposed and blood running down his chest. A slender piece of metal sticking out of the wound. He looked to be on his deathbed.

"Tyler!" Ed screamed.

One of the men who had brought Ed up cuffed him behind the ear.

"No, no, no," the man at the desk said. "Let him speak. Let him make his presence known." The man stood, walked over to Ed, and sat down on a chair that one of the men had placed for him.

"My name is Salazar. But I am going to assume you know that, just as I assume this here is your son."

Ed nodded.

"Good, see? We have started out well. Now, your son took something from me.

Something very important. Did he tell you about this?"

Ed thought about how to respond, but slowly nodded again. It was pointless to plead ignorance.

"Did he tell you what he did with it?"

"No."

"Tell you where it is?"

"No."

"Nothing?"

"No. He just told me what he did, nothing more."

"So he told you he stole from me, stole a large shipment, millions of dollars, and yet you helped him leave Mexico? Why? Why would you do this if he didn't tell you more?"

Edward considered his words. He was about to voice into existence the thoughts that he had kept buried in his mind.

"He is my son . . ."

"Yes, you said that."

"That is why."

Salazar stood and walked over to Tyler. He bent over and whispered in his ear. "Your father is a good man, eh? You see him there. Come all this way for his son. And this is his reward? Look at him," Salazar said. "Look at him!"

Tyler raised his head, his right eye gazing

at Edward.

"Where is my shipment!"

In Tyler's face, beneath the bruises, Ed could see fear, regret, failure. He could see his son shifting through the emotions and not able to come up with an idea of what to do. Tyler closed his eye and shook his head.

"*Acido!*" Salazar yelled at one of his men.

The man walked over to Ed and pulled a small vial out of his inner coat pocket. It was a dropper. Ed watched as the man twisted the container open, lifted the tube up, and placed it over the back of Ed's hand. Salazar gave a sign and the man squeezed the dropper. Liquid fell on Ed's skin and started to burn down through the layers.

74

Roberto counted the minutes as he hid himself away in one of the side rooms off the inner courtyard. Salazar's hacienda was massive, with staff wandering around every which way. Salazar had turned the Nuevo Negaldo plaza into his own little fiefdom. Many of the rising Cartel bosses became paranoid the higher they rose. Salazar was determined to be the exception to the rule, throwing lavish parties, flaunting his wealth and status. Even on the street, word was getting around that El Aguila was running out of patience with Salazar's exuberance.

That exuberance was going to be Salazar's Achilles' heel.

He had become soft with power. It was the reason why lowlifes like Tyler and Ignacio could rob from him. Salazar's reactions were always severe, but they were after the fact. He never saw the danger as it was standing right in front of him. Never saw how people would take advantage of his negligence and lack of foresight.

And now, as evening descended, with bats flying overhead and lights illuminating the courtyard, Roberto was using all of Salazar's faults to his advantage. He was in his mansion and he was ready to get his mother back.

From his pocket he pulled out Felipe's rosary and wrapped it around his wrist. The cross hung down and he clenched it in his fist. He looked at his other hand, the Lady of Guadalupe tattoo on his inner forearm, her hand lifted in blessing, her eyes looking down toward his own hand wielding the pistol.

Roberto had never been in Salazar's palace before, and he had no idea where to start looking. From his spot he cracked the door open and looked out. He saw two men walking on the upper walkway across the courtyard. They took an open stairway down to the first level, then through an archway and down below ground. Not knowing where to start, Roberto thought he might as well follow them. He stepped out, made his way to the landing, and then headed down the stairs. As they descended, the stairs circled to the left. He kept his shoulder to the wall, his weapon extended in his right hand as he ventured into the basement.

The men walked down a long corridor toward a door at the end, and then knocked on it. A few words were spoken, the door opened, and they disappeared inside.

Roberto stepped down the hall and put his ear to the door. Logic told him there were at least three inside, but he had no idea if there were any more. He listened, slowing his breath so as not to obscure his senses.

Through the door he heard the voices, muffled by the wood. Then he heard a slap and the scream of a woman. He knocked on the door and stepped back.

"Yes?"

"Salazar told me to come down here," Roberto said.

The door opened, and before the man on the other side knew what happened, a bullet entered his forehead. He fell backward and Roberto followed him inside. One man was standing in front of a woman tied to a chair, the other was sitting along the far wall. The man standing reached for a gun, but Roberto fired two shots and dropped him. Turning, he fired at the man who was seated and put two shots in him as well. It was over in less than seven seconds.

Roberto lowered his gun hand and clenched his left around the rosary.

He went over to the woman in the chair and began to untie her. Her reflexes forced her back in her seat and she started hyperventilating. Roberto tried his best to calm her. He took the hood off her head, and to his surprise, he had found what he had come for.

"Mama, it's me."

"Roberto?"

"Yes."

"Oh Roberto," Camilla sobbed. "Oh my boy, my son."

Roberto hushed her as he got the tape off her feet, and then her hands. "We have to get out of here. Quickly. Keep your eyes closed until we get to the hallway."

"Why?"

"I don't want you to see this."

She did as he told her and kept her eyes shut. Roberto guided her out of the room, down the hallway, and cautiously up the stairs. Once he knew it was clear, they went across the courtyard back to the empty room that he had hidden in previously. When they were inside and the door was closed, Camilla wrapped her arms around her boy and was on the verge of weeping.

"What is happening?"

"I'm sorry, Mama. I let this happen. This is my fault."

"They were asking about you. And about Tyler. His father was in the same room as me not more than a half hour ago."

"They're here?"

"Yes."

The man he saw being taken upstairs must have been Tyler's dad. Roberto stepped away from his mother and, for the first time that day, wondered what he would do next.

75

Now in the relative safety of the room off the courtyard, Camilla let her emotions finally take hold of her. She grabbed Roberto and held him tight. Her tears came to the surface, and she cried out the fear that had held her in its grip since Lomas had taken her from the motel. She cried also in relief as she held her son in her arms, thankful that he was still alive.

"Mama, it's okay," Roberto said.

She squeezed him again and then stepped back, wiping her eyes and regaining her composure.

"We're getting out of here. It won't be long until they find the bodies in the basement."

"But . . . Edward is here . . ."

Roberto stared back at her, but his face was cold.

"We can't just . . . leave . . . ," she said. She had no idea what to do next. Everything in her told her to run, but leaving an innocent man behind to be killed, coupled with her sense that she was powerless to do anything to stop it, froze her in place.

"What do you expect me to do?"

"I don't know, Roberto."

"I'm here to save you."

"Yes, but what will we be if we just leave him?"

Roberto put his hands up to his head. The pistol in one hand, the rosary in the other. His frustration was apparent, but as she looked at him, she saw that he too was wrestling with the choice. There he was again, the good son. He wasn't gone. Not yet. Her words still found their way into a sliver of his conscience that he had failed to bury.

"You know, Mama, we are here right now because I did just what you are saying. He is up there because I saved Tyler. That was a mistake."

"No, Roberto. That was no mistake."

"It was. It was a mistake. His life is less to me than yours."

"And yours to mine, which is why it was no mistake. The man I know you are is what saved him. Not this cholo mask you wear. You did the right thing. I pray for you to do the right thing all the time, Roberto. But for us to leave, to turn our backs on them — that was the mistake, and I was the one to make it. I thought I could save us by going along. By telling them what they wanted. But no. There is no dealing with evil."

"They are gringos, Mama. What mercy have they ever shown us?"

"It makes no matter," she said. She reached out and grabbed her son's hand. She held it close, pulled open his fist that clenched the rosary, and looked at it.

"Felipe's, yes?"

Roberto nodded.

"His death is not your fault."

Camilla could see tears forming in her son's eyes.

"You hear me? It is not your fault. Felipe would have helped anyone who asked for it. Even if he knew it would end like this. He would have done it and not wavered from helping. It was who he was. His blood is not on your hands, but his blood is in you."

She closed his hand around the rosary again and brought it to her lips and kissed his hand. She looked at her boy, put her hand up to his face, and caressed his cheek.

"Whatever happens now, it is not on you. My life is my choice, just as yours is yours. I will not leave him here. Though I do not know what to do."

Roberto breathed deeply. He stepped back from her, his armor going back up.

"Alright, Mama. Alright," he said. "For Felipe."

She smiled despite the fear. "For Felipe."

"Stay hidden," he said. "Stay safe."

She nodded.

He left the room and made his way across the courtyard toward the stairs.

76

"You see, Tyler. We will take your father a piece at a time," Salazar said.

Ed heard the words spoken across the room, but his mind could not focus on anything other than the shooting pain in his body. The backs of his hands were on fire, the chemical eating away at the flesh and melting the tissue. The back of his fists bearing the mark of the sins of his child. He could not think. The only thing racing through his mind was the searing agony of his body. He screamed through the bit that Salazar's men had forced into his mouth and his feet kicked at the floor.

"Just tell me where my shipment is and I will stop this. It's that easy," Salazar said, his frustration evident, simmering below the surface.

Tyler's head lay limp to one side, the swelling continuing to increase from the beating he received earlier, but there was a slight movement of assent at Salazar's words and the room fell silent.

"Yes?" Salazar said. "You tell me, and there will be no more of this."

Tyler's words were barely audible and Salazar leaned down to hear. As he did so, Tyler raised his head and bit into Salazar's ear with the viciousness of a lunatic. Ed's own muffled whimperings were drowned out by the screams of Salazar, who managed to pull himself away from Tyler by leaving a part of himself behind. The goons ran over and started beating Tyler again.

The vision of his son being hit, Salazar bleeding from his wound, combined with his own torment, were enough to drive Ed to the brink of insanity.

"Enough!" Salazar yelled. "Don't kill him. I need to know where it is."

Then, to add to the chaos filling the room, the sound of gunfire from outside the mansion echoed through the air and then went silent. Silence filled the room as each person tried to process what they just heard.

In agony, Salazar walked over to his desk, put the phone to his good ear, and spoke into it. He spoke again. There was no one on the other end.

"Go down and see what is happening!" he yelled at his men. They left together, and from a desk drawer Salazar pulled out a large pistol.

This is it, Ed thought, and as the pain from the chemical burns torched away his resolve, there was a part of him that almost welcomed it.

More gunfire came from outside, closer. Salazar was visibly shaken, not just from the wound on his ear, but from whatever was erupting outside. There were two loud thuds and the sound of bodies rolling down stairs. From farther away, more gunshots. It was as if the entire hacienda was under attack. And then through the open doorway a man appeared.

His presence was like an avenging angel incarnate. Stoic, his arm raised confidently, a holy relic dangling from the other.

Roberto.

His gun was aimed straight at Salazar, with Ed and Tyler strapped in between the two gunslingers.

77

El Matacerdos had awoken and gathered his things. He had slept longer than expected and evening was encroaching on the border city. He left the hotel room, put the duffel back in the trunk, and set off for Salazar's mansion. The streets leading to the hillside were clearing out as the cautious and respectable were preparing dinners. The city in his rearview mirror glowed as the sunset of the high desert filled his windshield. He took the gravel turnout that led to Salazar's place. He parked the car on the road and headed up the drive to the gate. The only sound came from the stones crunching under his feet. It was as if he were the only man left on earth.

Approaching the gate, he saw the man sitting in the guard booth, watching something on his phone. Earbuds in his ears, soccer highlights on the screen, he took no notice of the man outside his booth. El Matacerdos raised his right arm and fired one round into the man's head, entered the booth, and pushed the button to open the gate. He took a radio off the man, put it on his belt, and walked into the compound.

Hearing the gate open, another man appeared at the entrance of a garage and El Matacerdos quickly dispatched him. This man's execution didn't go unnoticed as his comrade came out of the same structure and started firing haphazardly. Another round and this man was down, but the alarm was raised.

Now, it was just fate and accuracy.

El Matacerdos went up the tiered entry to the front door of the mansion. When it opened, he fired instinctively, and the look on the man's face was both one of surprise and pain. He fell backward, his hand still on the door handle, swinging it open, and the sicario stepped over him into the house.

Shouts came from all corners of the hacienda as men emerged from doors and stairwells. He took them all down, their shots were those of lazily trained soldiers, his of expertise. He was efficient with each shot, slipping in a new clip when one went empty.

Soon it was quiet.

From the top of the stairs leading up to

the second story, El Matacerdos saw two men roll down the steps. These were not his kills. He walked over and examined them. Two close-range bullet holes in the men's heads.

He went up the stairs, unaware of the worried eyes of a woman peering at him from a side room off the courtyard.

Camilla watched the firefight with both fear and awe. The assassin who entered the house dealt with each of Salazar's men like a man swatting at flies. She watched as the scene calmed and the assassin made his way across the courtyard, the smell of gunpowder and a haze of smoke obscuring his movements. He approached the stairway, bent down to look at two of the dead men, and then went up the steps.

To where Roberto was.

Her heart skipped a beat.

She opened the door, ran across the courtyard, and mounted the stairs. From there she screamed at the top of her lungs — a warning of the deadly figure coming up after her son.

"Roberto!"

78

The events that happened next would become fodder for narco-corridos all across Mexico. The boys in Los Diablos would be riding in their cars, listening to the singer croon about one of their own and the shootout at Salazar's plaza.

The gunfight lasted less than a few seconds, the narco songs a hundred times longer, but for Roberto, the scene stretched to a slow infinity as each of his senses took in every aspect of the action.

Roberto had taken several steps into the room and sidestepped away from the door. His gun hand was raised. His other gripped the memory of his uncle. The gringos were tied up facing each other, both battered and bruised by the torture of Salazar and his thugs.

Salazar drew his pistol and aimed it at him. Roberto fired first, but the mixture of adrenaline and vengeance caused his aim to not be true, his shot hitting Salazar in the shoulder. Salazar fired wide, the momentum of Roberto's bullet knocking him off balance.

From outside the room a woman screamed. It was Camilla.

Distracted, Roberto turned to the door and saw a man dressed in black, hair black, his face in shadow and cold like onyx. The man had his gun raised, but it wasn't pointed at Roberto, it was pointed at Salazar.

Fire erupted in Roberto's side. A bullet ripped into his abdomen. In the split second his eyes were averted, Salazar had shot him.

The man in the doorway fired, dropping Salazar with a cluster of rounds to the chest.

Roberto watched as Salazar fell behind his desk. He himself fell to the floor and the blood started to seep from his side. He watched as the man entered the room, his heavy boots echoing on the floor, sending the sound into Roberto's ear, resonating through the tiles. The man walked over to where the plaza boss lay. He fired two quick shots.

Salazar was dead.

Felipe was avenged. It didn't matter who had fired the fatal round.

Roberto felt hands reach below his arms

and turn him on his back. It was his mother. She rolled him onto her lap, her tears streaming down her face. She rocked him.

The man walked over to her, his gun still raised.

"Who is he?" he asked, pointing his gun down at Roberto.

"He is my son," Camilla said, rocking her boy.

"And them?" he said, nodding to Tyler and Edward tied in the chairs, their own wounds leaking onto the floor.

"Them?"

"Yes."

"Familia."

The man thought about it and then gave her a short nod. He holstered his gun and left the room.

Camilla wiped the brow of Roberto with one hand, her other hand on his across his heart. He was drifting away from her.

"I'm scared, Mama."

"I know, Roberto . . ."

"Take my phone," he struggled to say. "Call Adan. He will get you out. Go away from here. It is death here."

She squeezed him tighter as his breaths became shorter.

"Please, Mama. Do not stay in Nuevo

Negaldo. Leave this place."

"I will. We both will. We will leave together."

"No, Mama. I think I'm staying here. With Felipe."

She clenched her teeth, fighting the urge to scream to God.

Roberto looked up, away from Camilla, then closed his eyes. "Forgive me."

Who Roberto asked forgiveness of, they did not know. His mother? God? But as the rosary fell to the floor, Roberto left this world, and Camilla wept.

79

"It's done."

"Good. Did you take care of all of Salazar's men?"

El Matacerdos thought about the woman holding the dying man in her arms. How that man had been in the room attempting to kill Salazar. How the woman's eyes spoke to him and caused him to stay his actions. He would keep that incident to himself. The man was dying, the woman would be gone. The two men tied up, her familia she had said, were obviously not with Salazar.

"Yes," he said.

"I need you here in Chihuahua. Leave Nuevo Negaldo immediately."

El Matacerdos walked out through the gate, got into his car, and headed south. In his mind, the eyes of the woman stared deep into his soul.

In shock, Camilla laid her boy down on the

tile, kissed his forehead, and prayed. She took the rosary from his hand and held it close to her lips. She wanted to lie down and die beside him. Before her, she saw his whole life, beginning and end.

She rose and untied Ed, and then Tyler. She did not speak to them. Words were lost to her as she returned to Roberto. Ed went to his own son. He looked at the piece of metal sticking out of the bullet wound. Quickly he grasped it and pulled it out, flinging it across the room. They all sat in the room, knowing they should leave, but lacking the strength and energy to move.

Eventually, Ed rose, walked over to Camilla, and knelt beside her. With Tyler's feeble help, they managed to carry Roberto's body down the stairs, through the courtyard, and out the front door. Bodies lay all about them as they walked toward the road.

Camilla did make the call to Adan, and Adan and Los Diablos came through. They picked up all four of them at the gates to Salazar's hacienda and drove them back to the garage. A doctor came in and treated both Ed's and Tyler's wounds. Adan then put the gringos in a car and sent them all the way to Nogales in the west. Once there, Ed and Tyler were pushed through the border crossing without question, thanks to the aid of one of Adan's cousins who was working the lanes that day.

Ed and Tyler took the bus east to Deming where another one of Adan's underlings had dumped Ed's truck. Together they started the drive back to Kansas.

Roberto's body, along with Felipe's, was shipped off to Juarez to be buried in a family plot, all at Adan's expense. Camilla kissed Adan on the cheek as she got into her car to follow the transport of her dead family.

"Thank you, Adan."

"I do this for Roberto. He should have come to me first."

"Would you have helped him?"

He didn't answer her question. "Now, do as he said, and don't come back."

She nodded, and pulled onto the eastern road.

Ed, Tyler, and Camilla all left on the eve of Nuevo Negaldo's plunge into a blood bath that would last for months. With Salazar dead, there was a power vacuum, or so the rival cartels thought. El Aguila put his most ruthless lieutenant in charge, who met the assault from the outsiders with so much depravity that the streets ran red with the blood of dead men. By El Día de los Muertos, many of Nuevo Negaldo's young men were dead, including countless members of Los Diablos, and eventually, Adan himself.

Adan died in his garage, at his table, counting the profits he made in a city under siege. No one would ever know who killed him. The police force, half butchered by the fall, was no longer investigating homicides. Adan's knowledge of Tyler and Edward died with him, and their tale became lost to the history of the drug war, buried in a million other stories of murder, thievery, and betrayal.

And the shipments still came north.

And the immigrants still came north.

And the killings continued until everyone who cared about what happened that previous summer was gone and new guns sought out new targets and new victims.

And out in the desert, in an old mine, beneath a canvas tarp, sat a truck that had been abandoned with a load that could make a poor thug rich, and for which so many people had died.

80

Agent Lomas perused the morning news-paper with a shaking hand. He had read the briefings earlier through work, heard the word from his network south of the border, but seeing it made public in print brought it home in a new way. He felt exposed and somehow more vulnerable than he did when word came down through the Agency that things were heating up in Nuevo Negaldo.

What shook him up the most was that there was no word, on the street or at work, about two gringos being found at Salazar's compound. It seemed unlikely that Salazar would have extracted what he needed and dumped the bodies between the time that Lomas had delivered them and the assault on his compound. The fact that there was no mention of two Americans dying in the drug wars, something that the papers and national television would blow out of pro-portion, is what made him nervous. If they were out there, all they had to do was tell someone in any agency what he had done and his whole charade would go down in flames.

But he was stuck.

He wanted to go south and look for them, to take action rather than just sit at home waiting. But he couldn't go down to Nuevo Negaldo. The purging of Salazar's organization was in full swing. He'd be marked as soon as he crossed over.

Stuck.

Wait here in El Paso for the authorities to come and indict him or cross over and let the Cartel end it all. He couldn't go to prison.

He wouldn't go to prison.

He put the paper down and sipped his coffee. The doorbell rang and his jittery hands spilled the mug's contents onto the table. He got up, went to the door, and looked through the peephole. It was just the mailman.

"Yes?"

"Package for you, Mr. Lomas."

"Just leave it at the door."

"You sure?"

"Yes, leave it."

"Okay."

The mailman did as he was told and left

the package.

His cell phone rang on the table where he had left it by the coffee mug. His heart was racing. He looked at the number. It was work.

"Lomas, wondering if you could swing by the office today. Something has come up with the situation in Nuevo Negaldo that I would like your opinion on."

It was his boss. His official boss.

Not Salazar.

Salazar was already dead. Lomas thought the drug lord lucky in that respect.

"Is it urgent?"

"A bit. Just come down when you can. Thanks."

The phone went dead.

They knew of his involvement. Edward and Tyler had shown up and spilled their story. He had used the same tactic in the past and he was not about to let it be played on him. He had to leave. He had to get out of El Paso. He would decide on the road he would take, but for now, he had to move.

Lomas went to his bedroom and packed a quick bag, clothes, toiletries, a jacket. He tucked his firearm into his shoulder harness and went to the front door. He looked outside and saw an empty street, save for the mailman who was now delivering at the

379

end of the block. He went outside, locked up the house, got into his car, and backed down the driveway.

He pulled down the street and thought about calling back into the office, making up an excuse that would buy him more time to disappear. He pulled out his cell phone, his other hand on the wheel, as he approached the stop sign at the end of the block.

Distracted by his hurried departure, he did not see the car pull up beside him.

He didn't see the gun pointed at his window.

His peripheral vision barely caught the blast of the shot as his window shattered, his left temple exploded, and the world went dark.

Later that day, a car crossed the border in Juarez and proceeded southwest toward Nuevo Negaldo. The two men inside, now safely back on the right side of the wire, headed to Nuevo Negaldo, eager to make a name for themselves with the new plaza boss.

81

Ed pulled into the driveway of the house in Jennison and shut the truck off. Tyler was in the passenger seat, the swelling on his face subsiding, the bruises turning a deep purple. His eyes were looking at the house he had not seen in years. Ed could only imagine what thoughts might be going through his son's head. Ed caught his own reflection in the rearview mirror and was reminded that he looked very similar to Tyler.

They hadn't talked much on the way home once they got the truck in Deming. Each to their own thoughts, Ed found himself constantly waiting for the other shoe to drop. A car of Cartel assassins behind them, a gunman at the rest area, a sicario emerging from the bathroom at the gas station, but none of these things happened. But he couldn't shut off his mind to the thoughts.

The road back to Kansas stretched out and condensed in a paradox of time. The miles whipped by even as the memory of Mexico moved in slow motion through his mind. Cars passed, the drivers innocent to the war that he had been through. Their naïve lives went on. Ed would always view his life differently. Every shadow, every noise, unexpected sensation would bring with it a twinge of fear, his nerves heightened and ready for flight.

When he pulled into Jennison and started looking for boogeymen around every corner, he realized these feelings would haunt him for years to come.

The house seemed smaller with the two of them in it. It was still in disarray from the ransacking it took before he left for New Mexico.

"Place is a mess," Tyler said.

"Yup."

"Salazar's guys?"

"Yup."

Tyler's shoulders slumped as if realizing that his actions had brought chaos to yet another part of the world. Ed started picking up the stuff on the living room floor, sifting through what was broken and what was still salvageable. Tyler walked over and started helping. They returned to silence until the first floor was somewhat livable again and evening was setting in.

"Your old room still has the bed in it," Ed said.

"Alright."

"You can stay as long as you want."

"You sure about that?"

"Yes."

"Thanks."

Tyler turned and took a few steps up the stairs, paused, and then looked back at his dad. "I don't know why you came down to Mexico, but I'm glad you did."

Edward thought about the words. He didn't know what had moved him to begin the journey that almost cost him his life, to try to save a son he had written off years before, a son whose own actions and criminal mind had caused a war to erupt in a border town and the death of countless people. For his part, he doubted he had contributed anything to the miracle of their escape. He was lost across the border, he lagged on the trail, cowered in the basement of Salazar's hacienda, and was strapped to a chair while a gunfight erupted around him. In fact, Tyler's fortunes would have ended the same whether he was there or not.

"I really didn't do anything."

"You were there, you know. I'm just glad

you were there."

"Get some sleep," Ed said.

Tyler went up to his old room and shut the door while Ed went to the fridge, managed to find a beer behind some food that had gone bad, and then made his way to the porch. He sat down in his chair, the sun setting in the west, and wondered at just what he had been through.

He looked down at his hands as one gripped the armrest and the other the bottle. The marks on them would probably last the rest of his life. The skin felt tight when he squeezed his fingers, the scar tissue glossy and smooth compared to the weathered leather. They would be visual reminders of his descent into the abyss.

He rocked and the door opened. Tyler stepped out onto the porch and leaned against the railing, looking out to the fields that he used to disappear into when he was a boy.

"Can't sleep."

Ed didn't say anything.

"Place hasn't changed much, has it?"

"I don't know. It didn't seem like it did, until now. Now it seems . . . smaller."

Tyler turned to his father and listened.

"I guess my mind isn't the same. This place was quiet. Solid. Perhaps I was fool-

ing myself my whole life as to what the world was like. Who knows? I'm just staring down the drive now, waiting for a car of lowlifes to drive up and take us back. It's like, once being part of it, I have this fear of being dragged back in."

"Well, you don't need to worry. You're back home. It's over."

"You think this is over?" Edward asked.

"Isn't it? Salazar is dead. So is everyone else. What's left?"

"Something buried out in the desert."

Tyler straightened a bit. Not much, but Edward saw it. That same tic every boy makes when they feel their inner conniving being sniffed out by a parent.

"That load you stole. Whatever it is, it's still out there, isn't it."

"Possibly."

"It is. Don't lie to me. Not now. Not after everything we've been through. I think I deserve the truth."

"Should still be out there. Like I said, everyone who knows about it is dead."

"You really believe that?" Ed said. He stood up, went inside, and came back with the phone. "Here, why don't you call the DEA or FBI or someone and tell them where it's at, let them go pick it up."

"Now? It's already late."

"Just get it off your chest."

"Tomorrow, Dad."

"Now, Tyler."

Tyler pushed the phone away and stepped back into the house, went up the stairs, and into his room. The door shut behind him and he didn't come back out. Edward finished his beer, locked up the house, and called it a night. The same old estrangement between him and his son slowly creeping back into the home.

When he woke in the morning, Tyler was gone.

82

The park in Hermosillo was quiet. El Matacerdos sat on a bench, his eyes searching his
surroundings at every car and passerby. Attack could come from any direction at any
time. It was never safe to meet like this, he
knew that. His old mistress sat in a car in
front of the store. The young boy jumped
out and went inside for a treat. El Matacerdos had already paid for the raspados, had
paid for treats for anyone who might have
gone into the store between noon and two,
just to make sure the owners couldn't tie
the boy to him.

Soon, the boy came out with a cup and
walked across the park. He sat down on the
other end of the bench and took a mouth-
ful. His eyes never landed on his father. He
had been trained, schooled in the art of
public meetings.

"How is school?" El Matacerdos asked.

"It's fine," the boy said.

"And your mother? Are you doing what she asks you to do?"

"Yes, Papa."

"Good."

"Where have you been?"

"You know you are not supposed to ask me these things."

The boy looked down to his cup and scraped the wooden spoon around the edges. He had finished too soon. He would have to pretend to eat phantom ice cream for as long as he wanted to sit next to his father.

"Do you not want to be with me, Papa?"

"More than anything."

"But the monsters won't let you?"

"I leave to keep the monsters away. If I stay, they could show up here and hurt you. I will never let that happen."

"Can't someone else fight them?"

"No, Pepe. Once you start, you cannot stop. I didn't know this when I started. Before you were born. If I had, well, I don't know. But I must keep them away."

"People ask where my papa is," the boy said casually.

"And what do you tell them?"

"That he is in the north. Like the others."

"Did you come up with that?" El Matacerdos asked.

The boy nodded as he continued to scrape the empty container. El Matacerdos smirked.

"You are a smart boy. Go on now, your mother is waiting."

"Will I see you soon?"

"Yes, soon."

"Okay, Papa."

The boy stood and hesitated. He turned slightly, stole a quick glance at his father, and smiled. Then he walked across the park to the waiting car. A twinge of deep sadness passed through El Matacerdos. He had taught the boy he could never hug him in public. The life he had sentenced them both to.

El Matacerdos watched the car pull away from the curb and drive off. He sat there for another half hour before he got up and walked to his own car parked a few blocks away.

83

The bell over the door to the appliance shop rang and Edward's heart skipped a beat. He doubted that would ever change. The feeling of dread at a familiar sound, a sound that for most of his life had been a welcoming chime, now caused a negative Pavlovian reaction in his gut. A part of him thought that someday another crew of hitmen would walk through that door. He would stand from his desk, walk out of the back room, and see an elderly townie still content to have an old machine serviced rather than buy a new one.

Today, it was no townie.

Camilla stood inside the door.

His heart quickened, but not in terror. He felt a smile cross his lips.

"Wow, it's good to see you," he said as he walked toward her. He didn't know whether to hug her or extend his hand, and he was stuck between the two gestures.

She read his intentions and gave him a hug. "You too."

"I never thought . . ." He tripped over his words. "What brings you to Jennison?"

"I came to see you."

Ed's words left him again.

"Is there a place we can talk?" she asked.

Ed looked at her and then rubbed his hands on his shirt. He suddenly realized how dirty he was.

"Sure. We can go across the street. Grab some coffee."

Camilla nodded.

"Just let me close up real quick," he said.

Ed grabbed his keys, flipped the Open sign over, and locked the door behind him. They walked over to the small eatery across the road, sat down at a booth, and waited for the waitress to bring them their drinks before another word was spoken.

"How are you doing?" Ed asked, not really knowing what to say.

"I'm making it, day by day. I miss him."

Edward listened without interruption.

"I haven't been back to Nuevo Negaldo. I do not think I ever will. Too many ghosts there for me. I sometimes think I never should have gone there to begin with. But where else could we have gone? He was so little then. I thought that he would be safe, you know? Safe because he was mine. My son. That my will for him would guide him. But, as with all boys, he was his own. He chose his own destiny.

"There is no one but me who knows the real Roberto. Remembers the real Roberto. The person he was deep down inside. The boy who would kiss his mother every night before going to sleep. Sometimes sneaking out of his bed to kiss me again. The man who was violent to the world but shielded his mother from danger. I am the only one who knows who he really was. It's lonely."

Edward reached out across the table and grasped Camilla's hand. "I saw him. I saw that part of him too."

Camilla smiled and wiped her eyes. She brought the coffee cup up to her lips and took a sip. Putting the drink down, she took a deep breath and smiled. "Thank you. I think that's why I came. Hoping to find that I was not the only one."

"Where will you go?"

"I don't know. There is nowhere to go back to."

He didn't know what he wanted her to say, but Edward wanted her to stay. Like her, there was no one who understood what he had been through. No one to talk to. That's the one thing about a shared history.

It forever binds two people together.

"And where is Tyler?" she asked.

"Gone."

She nodded, this time it was her who reached out for his hand. Her thumb ran over the scarring on the back of his hand.

"I guess, I don't know," he said. "I thought that after everything, he'd change. Get smart. Realize something. But after we got back home, he was gone the next morning. It makes me wonder why I even bothered in the first place. I got suckered again."

"No," she said. "You weren't. You did the right thing. For our children, we simply do. Not for the reward. Not for something down the line. Simply for doing."

He looked at her. She was truth and mystery all rolled up in one.

84

Ed had invited Camilla over for dinner, which she accepted. They sat in the kitchen making small talk, eating, and taking their time. It was nice to have someone in the house who talked with him. They did their best not to converse about Nuevo Negaldo, but as hard as they tried, the conversation always ended up there.

Camilla walked over to the couch while Ed began to clear the dishes. He turned on the TV, handed her the remote, and glanced at the screen as he picked up their plates. A small story ran across the ticker at the bottom, a major drug seizure out west.

Camilla glanced at Ed and flipped the channel.

Ed put the leftovers in the fridge, and as he closed the door, his eyes fell on the card hanging there under the magnet. The card the desert priest passed out. Toribio Romo. It was now a relic reminding him of things he both wanted to forget and to remember.

His hands in the sink, scrubbing dishes, he let his thoughts wander as he looked out the kitchen window, across the plains to the southwest, toward the memories that haunted him. Somewhere out there were men lying in a rocky crag, gazing up at the stars. Men sleeping in shacks, waiting for trucks to carry them north. Men walking through wilderness, blind to the paths and futures ahead of them.

Somewhere out there was Tyler.

He was drying his hands when he thought he heard a knock on the door. His stomach clenched, the ever-present dread rising. He sucked in a deep breath and went to open the door.

Tyler stood there on the porch.

"You mind if I crash here for a while?"

Ed looked at his son. He had no idea if he would be here tomorrow, or the next day, or any day after that. But for now, here he was. And he was willing to take it for what it was.

"Yeah," Ed said. "I'd like that."

Dunn Public Library

ACKNOWLEDGMENTS

Many thanks to Andrea, for pushing me to complete this story, conceived several years ago. To the most incredible editor, Barb, everything you fix is magic. To Michele and Hannah, thanks for all your work getting books into as many people's hands as possible.

To all the family, friends, and old schoolmates who have supported me over the past several years. I could never show enough appreciation for the encouragement you have shown.

And lastly, to Liz. You are the source of all good things for me. Thank you for an incredible life.

ABOUT THE AUTHOR

Samuel Parker was born in the Michigan boondocks but was raised on a never-ending road trip through the US. Besides writing, he is a process junkie and the ex-guitarist for several metal bands you've never heard of. He lives in West Michigan with his wife and twin sons.

The employees of Thorndike Press hope you have enjoyed this Large Print book. All our Thorndike, Wheeler, and Kennebec Large Print titles are designed for easy reading, and all our books are made to last. Other Thorndike Press Large Print books are available at your library, through selected bookstores, or directly from us.

For information about titles, please call:
(800) 223-1244

or visit our website at:
gale.com/thorndike

To share your comments, please write:
Publisher
Thorndike Press
10 Water St., Suite 310
Waterville, ME 04901